ISBN: 978-0-9766231-8-2
Published by Kerri Hawkins and Red Raptor Productions.
ZEN 12, Vol 1, 2016. FIRST PRINTING.
Office of Publication: Long Beach, California
ZEN 12, its logo, all related characters and their likenesses are ™ and © and ™ 2016
Kerri Hawkins and Red Raptor Productions.

What did you think of this book? We love to hear from our readers.
Please email us at: khawkins@bloodlegacy.com.

ZEN 12

by Kerri Hawkins

Also from Kerri Hawkins

THE STORY OF RYAN
BLOOD LEGACY I
(ISBN: 978-0-9766231-7-5)

THE HOUSE OF ALEXANDER
BLOOD LEGACY II
(ISBN: 978-0-9766231-0-6)

HEIR TO THE THRONE
BLOOD LEGACY III
(ISBN: 978-0-9766231-1-3)

ORIGIN OF SPECIES
BLOOD LEGACY IV
(ISBN: 978-0-9766231-5-1)

visit us on the web at
www.bloodlegacy.com

CHAPTER 1

GARRETT REMEMBERED THE FIRST TIME she saw it and truly understood what was coming. She was sitting in a restaurant, back when they still had restaurants, when there were still waitresses and waiters, a human being who came and asked you what you wanted.

She was sitting in a fully packed diner and it was eerily quiet. A clank of silverware and the rattling of dishes would drift out from the kitchen, but beyond that, it was almost silent. Fifty people sat in that room, many across from each other, their heads bent reverently as if in prayer. They did not speak to one another and they ate mindlessly. There was only the tapping of keyboards, the subtle sound of the pads of fingers on touchscreens.

Garrett looked around the room. At the time, the "zombie apocalypse" was fashionable in popular culture, endlessly harvested in the media of that era. But the apocalypse had already occurred; people just didn't realize it. The zombies had already been victorious in a bloodless coup. No violence had been necessary, and no one seemed to miss their brains.

Garrett's own phone, that anachronistic world-altering object, was sitting on the table next to her elbow. She felt anxious at what she was about to do, untethering herself, cutting the cord wrapped about her neck so she could breathe freely for a few months. Well, six months at the most, according to her doctor.

The screen was warm, soothing. Garrett's fingers caressed the smooth outlines of the artistically designed casing. It was a marvel of engineering, a model of artisan craftsmanship. The screen was beautiful, packed with colors. She toyed with the recessed button, then slowly, infinitesimally began to apply pressure. The screen blinked at her uncertainly, surprised, even shocked. Was she certain? Had she pressed the wrong button? Perhaps she meant to watch a video instead?

She was certain. She continued to apply pressure until the screen faded, as if she were slowly choking the life from it, and then it went to black.

No alarms were sounded. No one looked up. No one seemed to have even noticed, which for some reason surprised Garrett. She paid the bill with US money, another anachronism. She passed a homeless bum who stood outside the diner, thrusting out his filthy hand for whatever someone might throw in his direction. It struck Garrett that he was the only one she had seen who was truly "there," which is why she had mixed emotions about her next act. She handed him the phone, uncertain if she was bestowing on him a gift or a curse. Perhaps he would sell it, but Garrett doubted that as he was already turning it on as she walked away.

That act would change everything in her life. Not the act of giving the phone away, but rather the simple act of turning it off. Garrett did not die six months later, or six years later, or even sixty years later. She volunteered for a bizarre and ill-fated research experiment involving telomerase that would end in catastrophe. The initial trials with small animals and primates had been so promising. But 499 out of 500 research subjects died horribly in phase one of the experiment.

Except Garrett. She lived on, the cancer that had been eating her from the inside out suddenly and mysteriously gone. For ten years she allowed them to study her, to poke and prod and try to figure out why she was different, why she had survived when no one else had. The fact that she was not aging became apparent as the years went by, exciting even more speculation and calls for research.

But Garrett was finished and walked away from all of it, just like she walked away from her phone.

CHAPTER 2

"WE HAVE A DISTURBANCE IN Sector 46-G-52-1."

The voice entered directly into Garrett's head. She concentrated briefly and the information screen appeared about a meter in front of her face. She bumped the opacity down so she could still see the room behind it, noting that Zen 64 and Zen 82 were both receiving the same message.

"Let me guess," Garrett said, recognizing the designated sector, "more Amish on Raider violence?"

Zen 64, a jovial giant of a man also known as Mike, chuckled. "I don't know who designed the grid in that location, but that was some poor decision-making." His pearly white teeth contrasted sharply with his pitch black skin. Although racial designations were still used when Garrett was young, the explosion of diversity and intermarriage made them more and more confusing. It was not unusual for someone to have such mixed heritage it made no sense to call them anything. When you're Caucasian-Asian-African-Indian-Latino, well, really, you're not anything at all. Technology, of course, then made the designations completely irrelevant as people saw what they wanted to inside the grid.

Mike, however, at least to Garrett's eye, was someone who truly could be called black, not as a racial category, but as a descriptor in the same way she could be called a very diluted, pale beige and Zen 82, also known as Charlene, could be called a deep caramel.

"And will the illustrious Zen 12 be accompanying us on this jaunt?" Mike teased.

Garrett sighed at the joke. She accompanied them on every field call, just as she always had. And Mike teased her, just as he always did because "Zen 12" was the oldest identification still on active duty. No one knew anything about Zen 1 through Zen 11. Zen 13 through, well, almost up to Mike's designation were assigned to administrative positions, were inactive, or were dead.

But Garrett still worked the field. And even though Mike, Charlene and Garrett had been partners for years, neither of them had any idea how old she really was. In reality, at this point in time, so many from her past had died that to her knowledge, only the Intermediary knew her actual age. The Intermediary was rather timeless and ageless herself, and Garrett had no idea of her true age. Although ultimately responsible for the management and governance of the grid, the Intermediary did not have a Zen designation. In Garrett's mind, she often thought of her as Zen 0.

Char punched Mike in the arm. "Of course the boss is going. The few times you and I go out alone, it always ends in disaster."

Mike sighed. "Sad but true." He winked at Garrett. "Ain't no one calmer, no one cooler under pressure."

"It's my years of experience," Garrett said with another sigh. "Did the disturbance begin in 52-1 or 52-2?" she asked, tilting her head to the side and addressing a point slightly above everyone's head in the room, deliberately looking at nothing. It was a standard gesture, considered polite and good etiquette so that no one else in the room mistakenly thought she was speaking to them. People who did not engage in such etiquette were referred to disparagingly as "bleeders," i.e. those who let their internal and external dialogues bleed together, causing confusion.

Zen 64 and 82 knew Garrett was addressing Central Communications, and the response was piped into the common channel.

"52-1," came the soothing female voice. It was only vaguely robotic, retaining just enough of that flavor for an appropriate level of professionalism.

"So it's on the Amish side," Char said, "damn I hate those outfits."

She stood. All three were dressed identically in gray and black form-fitting jumpsuits. From a distance, the material looked like cloth. Closer inspection, however, revealed hundreds of thousands of flexible nano-fibers woven together so that it was essentially a giant circuit board. The uniforms were similar in appearance to the gray and blue dress of every other member of the population. Theirs, however, were thickly armored and more functionally extreme than the civilian suit. The nano-fibers collected light, bending it, shaping it, creating any form of illusion desired.

"Do we have to go native on this one?" Mike asked, knowing the answer. "I look like a dick in that beard."

"Yes," Garrett said, "52-1 is an isolation sector. You know it's SOP to go in native and only go Guardian when we have to."

"Fuck," Char said, tilting her head and looking to the ceiling. "Access library, appropriate attire, Sector 46-G-52-1."

Her clothing blurred, shifted, then transformed. She was no longer wearing the gray and black jumpsuit, but rather a long black dress, white apron, and white hat. Mike laughed out loud.

"As many times I've seen you in that dress, it's still so damn funny."

"Fuck off, preacher boy, and get your beard on."

Mike, too, shifted his suit and he was now wearing the traditional Amish garb and beard. He was gigantic for an Amish and refused to change the color of his skin, which was not required by policy, so he cut quite an interesting figure.

It was now Garrett's turn. "I'm going to have to SC for this, you know the males won't recognize my authority while native."

"SC" was slang for sex-change. Gender in many ways had become as meaningless as race. However, in areas that requested and qualified for pure illusion, Garrett tried to adhere as closely as possible to local custom. She wasn't required to; Zen Guardians could go anywhere and do anything they wished within policy. But sometimes it was easier to accomplish goals by taking the path of least resistance.

The algorithms could somewhat change one's appearance, but they always held the seed of the original face. Garrett preferred to keep hers as close to her natural looks as possible, albeit male instead of female. "Activate SC, Amish attire, elder council member."

A flash of blue light bathed her body, then changed her outward appearance. She glanced down, then looked to Char to confirm the complete transition.

"You know, you make a pretty hot looking guy, boss. But that beard has got to go."

"Yeah," Garrett said, "the sooner we get this done, the sooner it's gone. Let's go."

The three hopped the light rail system. Private transportation no longer existed, other than for public safety and government officials. And when travel was for non-emergency purposes, they generally took public transportation. It gave them an opportunity to patrol different sectors while in camouflage.

The train was always an experience, as were all shared spaces of the grid. Over ninety-nine percent of the human population was now under the influence of augmented reality twenty-four hours a day. Ninety-nine percent of the one billion people left on earth lived in a world that did not actually exist, a world created by a computer that was overlaid on actual reality so that they could see and experience life any way they chose. It wasn't real, but no one cared anymore. After World War V, roughly half of the earth's land masses were no longer livable. What remained of the decimated populations congregated to the cities as a whole, desperate for any type of communal living.

Augmented reality was not new; it was already entrenched before the wars and disasters. But what it morphed into never could have been expected. It was initially a social experiment, a way of overlaying information onto places and things. But the information began to become the place, began to become the thing, and soon the places and things themselves became less interesting and eventually ceased to exist in any meaningful way.

The "grid" and "AR" were interchangeable terms, although in a technical sense, the grid was the physical hardware that ran the AR system. AR could be experienced in three ways. It could be experienced in isolation, in which a single person overlaid the theme they wished on whatever they were seeing. It could be experienced in groups in which the group as a whole shared and interacted within a theme. Or it could be turned off entirely, in which a person saw what was really in front of their eyes.

No one ever used option number three anymore. Well, no one except Guardians, and most of them did so only because it was part of their job. And Guardians alone had a most interesting option number four. Because it was their duty to maintain and protect the integrity of so many competing illusory worlds, they could also see what any given individual was seeing at any given time. Which is what made shared spaces so very interesting.

For a moment, as she often did, Garrett switched her visual plane off-grid. The interior of the car was very sterile, very plain, no adornment or decoration whatsoever. All of the occupants were dressed in identical blue and gray jumpsuits. Most were exceedingly plain and drab individuals, so little individuality amongst them they could have been automatons. Mike and Char were dressed in their Guardian uniforms, as was Garrett. No one on the train was aware that they were Guardians, although were any of them to go off grid for even a moment, that fact would immediately become known by their distinctive garb. But no one ever chose option number three anymore, not even for a second.

Garrett switched back to the shared channel, and Mike and Char were again dressed as Amish, as was everyone else on the train. They had not so much altered their appearance as aligned themselves with Sector 52-1's grid so that they would perceive and share the reality they lived in.

Garrett examined the other occupants of the train, always curious to see where or when they had chosen to live. A very pleasant looking, elderly lady sat in front of her. In the Amish reality, she was quietly humming while knitting a sweater. Garrett gave the mental command to shift to her reality, and was unsurprised to see she had turned back time to before the wars, to what she probably assumed was a happier era. This was very common in people who had grown up in ubiquitous AR, to choose the reminisces of someone else. They had no choice, because now no one had a life to remember, they had only memories of fabrications.

She moved to the man behind her, who had chosen a less mundane world in which to live. It looked to be around 19th century, mid-western United States. Everyone was dressed as a cowboy, and he himself bristled with six guns and a bandolier. He wore a marshal's badge on his chest and twirled the tips of his waxed mustache while he fingered his pocket watch.

Char and Mike were clearly engaged in the same activity as Garrett was.

"Uh oh," Mike said, "pervert on aisle 6."

Char and Garrett both switched to the indicated channel and burst out laughing. This was probably the most common reality they saw. It had many sordid nicknames, but its official title wasn't much better. It was known as Nudist Colony.

Everyone on the train was completely naked, including the man who sat with his legs spread wide as he gaped about at the imaginary nudity around him.

"Oh please," Char said, examining herself, "my breasts do not look like that."

"And why is my package so small?" Mike said, glancing down in dismay.

"You know the algorithms are always conservative with a small degree of randomness thrown in." Garrett glanced at the size of Zen 64's package. "That does look a little small for you."

"Thank you," Mike said indignantly, "I'm going to request the engineers re-seed the noise factor for the random generator on Nudist Colony. It's clearly generating unnatural results."

Garrett had to smile at the phrase. "Unnatural." None of this was natural. It could only be natural within its frame of reference, only be consistent within its theme.

As omnipresent as the grid was, it had its limitations. People could not just make up anything. The programming and processing power required to sustain and overlay even a single reality was enormous. The engineers solved that problem by providing broad themes for people to choose from. One could always make a request, within reason, and if there was sufficient demand for that theme, the overlay would be created. And the more information that was available, the more likely the project would be completed. If a time or place had a great deal of historical and cultural information available, a robust world could be manufactured and sustained. Garrett was always amazed at the number of people who chose to live in Ancient Greece, wandering about statuary wearing togas. They weren't actually ever in Greece; that island nation had ceased to exist and the entire Mediterranean was irradiated and would be uninhabitable for the next 245,000 years. But wherever these people were, well, it was Ancient Greece.

And the world that the theme was based on did not necessarily have to be "real," a term Garret admitted had become somewhat slippery. One of their most frequent calls involved disputes between the occupants of Starfleet Academy and those from the Jedi Training Center, not to mention the internecine disputes between the "Kirks" and the "Picards." That sector was one giant fiasco.

Garrett examined the various occupants of the train car. Some of the limitations of the grid were coded in on purpose because much of the early AR revolved around game programming and theory. Allowing individuals to change their appearance continually and without restriction would have broken the system. Changing the aggregate was easy in comparison. So an individual could somewhat change their appearance based on certain algorithms. They could make themselves slightly more or slightly less attractive, which, broken down into code, generally meant their features were more or less symmetrical, more or less proportional, and more or less interracial. Years of study had been distilled down into the rules universal attractiveness, which seemed to be consistent across almost all cultures. Humans liked symmetry, they liked proportion, they liked an "international" look, and they liked anything that represented fertility. Youth, of course, played into that latter category, and age was also something that could be altered. But again, the illusion could only be carried so far because the AR was merely laying on top of what was really there. It was generally recommended that one not alter one's age by more than plus or minus ten years because it began to strain the illusion. But, like the bad comb-over from years gone by, there were always those who pushed the envelope, wearing an illusion that looked like a 20 year-old while the body walked and talked like it was 50.

Garrett glanced around the train. She was always curious why the engineers included the "less attractive" option. Statistics showed that 96 percent of the people chose to make themselves more attractive, 3 percent chose to appear as they really were, and only 1 percent of the population chose to make themselves less attractive. Even those choosing to inhabit so-called post-apocalyptic realities wanted to look good in their hellish worlds A robust 99.6 percent of all males had chosen the penile enlargement option, and eventually a delimiter had to be coded into the system because there was too great of a disconnect between illusion and reality. It may have looked like 10 inches, but it didn't feel like 10 inches.

"I'm going back to 52-1," Garrett said, and Mike and Char transitioned back to their Amish garb while Garrett changed sexes once more. Interestingly, physical sex changes were less regulated than virtual ones.

The transgender trait in individuals was identified very young with an extraordinary degree of accuracy, and the appropriate surgical adjustments were made. A male who had transitioned to a female was forever identified with that biological sex, and vice versa.

Virtual sex changes, however, were not allowed in a casual sense. In the early stages of AR this prohibition had not been in place and it caused enormous conflict. The engineers had reasoned that many video game players explored virtual worlds as the opposite sex and therefore might want that option in "real" life. The problem was that there was no actual physical contact in the virtual world whereas most AR did in fact end in bed. It was one thing to have your pixelated avatar bopping a she-male, another thing entirely to physically experience this for yourself. After numerous encounters ended in violence, the engineers attempted to code in a number of safeguards. Although anyone could change their appearance, there was one spot on the body that could not be altered. It was affectionately referred to as the "Adam's apple" and it was conveniently located in the same vicinity on the jumpsuits, red for males, blue for females. So although anyone could appear as male or female, they could not hide their actual sex. Everyone had the option of ignoring the indicator on others if they chose, or even disabling the notification, but there were no unwelcome surprises.

The exceptions to this rule were Guardians in the line of duty. The indicator on Garrett's armor would change to red when she went SC, then to blue when she returned to normal.

Although people could flit about from theme to theme, they generally settled on one reality as their reality, even though it was never actually *the* reality. True, AR was now mature and well-established, but it suffered some early growing pains before standard rules were adopted. The first generation born into AR, when the law passed and the corneal implants became mandatory at birth, bore the brunt of those early mistakes. Some parents allowed their children freedom to experiment, and that had horrible results. Because of that, many parents chose not to tell their children about the grid at all until they were teenagers, which had even worse results. Twenty-three percent of those teenagers committed suicide upon learning that what they thought was real did not exist. It scarred a generation, and standard rules of education were put in place. Parents still had the ultimate say over what theme their children would live in, but the State required a step-by-step orientation to the grid at certain age-specific intervals.

"Come back, boss."

Mike drew Garrett from her reverie because the train was entering the station. Both Char and Mike were used to Garrett's endless bouts of reflection. The three exited onto a platform that was likely very plain, but to their eyes looked like something from the 1850s. Everything was finely crafted of wood, what metal was visible was simple and shaped by hand. There was little adornment, but the furniture had a hardy sturdiness to it and the building a clean architecture. The one thing that could not be hidden, however, was the "sponginess" of the ground, which seemed to give way with every step. There were plates beneath nearly every well-traveled surface, plates that absorbed and collected the kinetic energy of pedestrians as they walked across and compressed the surface. This station had the appearance of being devoid of technology, but that was an illusion on top of an illusion, because the technology to power the grid was woven into its very fabric, as it was everywhere.

Sector 52-G was within walking distance, which was good because Mike was none too fond of horses. A wagon with a happy Amish couple drove by, offering them a ride, but Garrett declined. The three Guardians appeared Amish to them, but that was because the Guardians had purposely altered their appearance and were sharing their grid. But everything else also looked Amish to the happy couple because that was how they chose to see the world. Even the Raiders that lived in the adjacent sector to them would look Amish. And conversely, the Amish would look like Raiders to the occupants of that sector, because that was the reality they chose to overlay on everything.

That was one of the tacit agreements to living within the grid: you could control how you saw everyone else and how you saw yourself, but you couldn't control how they saw you. True, your default appearance, i.e. the one that you decided upon, was largely retained regardless of what theme was overlaid upon you. This seemed strange to those who had not lived through the history of AR implementation, because why shouldn't you be able to see others any way you wanted when you could so change the world around you? But Garrett had been there through the chaos of this particular experimental phase. There were fads where everyone looked like a certain model or celebrity, and it was boring. If the changes to appearance were too bizarre it became wearying, unpredictable and jarring. Eventually, there was a complete loss of self, total disorientation when it no longer mattered how you saw yourself because it was in no way connected to how everyone else saw you. Additionally, too much energy was required to keep pace with the variability of this model. So the engineers maintained a default state of "self," even if that self was artificial and created. And each theme would statistically vary the template, but seeds of the original self would remain.

AR was most effective on a global scale and themes were much simpler to regulate, little more than a series of conditional statements and resultant function calls. If the Amish wanted Garrett to look Amish, she would look Amish. If the Raiders wanted her to look like a Raider, she would look like a Raider. If she went to the Aquarium Sector and they wanted her to look like a fish, she would look like a fish. But she would look like a Garrett fish, which in her case was exactly as she looked under normal circumstances since Garret was one of the 3% who had chosen not to alter her appearance. Guardians had the ability to override the overlay if it was necessary to maintain order, but most of the time it was simpler just to stay in character.

Certain groups chose to live within a shared reality, as the Amish did. Then everyone pretty much saw the same thing. And when such a group could demonstrate long-term cohesiveness, they could apply for an isolation permit. Isolation permits were rarely granted, and religious affiliation was the number one reason they were requested and approved. Requested, because each religion felt they needed to separate themselves from the unclean unbelievers surrounding them, and granted because the secularists in charge of the grid found that religious zealots were a pain in the ass and generally couldn't get along with anyone else.

The grid itself was not geographically confined. It could exist anywhere the infrastructure was in place, and it was in place in almost everywhere that was still inhabitable. Only Eastern China and the upper portion of North America, primarily the US and Canada, had emerged relatively unscathed from the world wars and then were able to survive the subsequent natural disaster that nearly destroyed the planet. Some of this was the luck of location, some of it was due to severe isolationist policies that both countries had adopted, and some was due to the back-dealing between the two nations that essentially sold everyone else out. But geography did not limit the grid.

Except in the case of an isolation permit. An isolation permit designated a discrete area in which only one manifestation of the grid was allowed. In Sector 52-G, everyone was Amish, everyone looked Amish, everyone saw Amish, and everyone acted Amish, whether they wanted to or not. For that reason, most people avoided going into isolation areas, other than for tourist-type excursions. No one was required to stay within an isolation area, but while inside of one, they were required to adhere to all local customs and mores.

The Guardians were approaching a small village and a group of men were engaged in a barn-raising. They all wore black pants and white shirts, their long sleeves rolled up in their exertion. A group of older men, probably the village elders, were standing off to the side, watching and giving direction. A group of women, all dressed in identical, ankle-length dresses and bonnets, sat off to the side engaged in various womanly projects. The younger women bowed their heads modestly when the young men tried to catch their eye.

"God I hate this world," Char murmured.

Garrett cleared her throat. It would not be professional to intrude upon their reality. She approached the group of elders, and a man with graying temples and a weathered face turned to greet her.

"Hail, strangers, are ye here for a visit to our fine town? Perhaps wishing to join our community?"

"No sir," Garrett said politely, "we are here on a different matter."

Just then, the village leader caught sight of Mike, who, although dressed in traditional Amish garb, looked nothing of the sort. His black skin was a stark contrast to the universally white population in front of him. He was also much larger than anyone present, and his muscles seemed to bulge from the black coat and pants, even though his clothing should have been as form-fitting as his suit.

"I see," the village elder said uneasily, his eyes returning to Garrett. "And how can we be of assistance to you?"

"We are here on a complaint, something regarding the neighbors."

The unidentified "we" in her statement increased the uneasiness of the entire group, and many of the men working on the barn stopped so they could overhear the conversation.

"We have not made any complaints about the neighbors," the elder said. "Although we consider them a strange lot, they generally keep to themselves."

"No," Garrett said patiently, "you don't understand. They have complained about you."

A large man with a reddish beard stepped forward and Garrett could feel Mike tense behind her.

"It's that little harlot, isn't it?" he demanded, "that little Jezebel!"

"Now Jeb," the elder said, trying to calm the red-haired man. "Keep your words peaceful."

"And what harlot would that be?" Garrett asked Jeb, her voice still neutral.

"My daughter, that's who!" Jeb spat out. "She disappeared last week, went over the border. I went to get her, to bring her home, and she refused."

Garrett could almost hear Char's eyes rolling in her head, but again she maintained complete neutrality.

"How old is your daughter?"

Jeb clenched his jaw, and Garrett knew the answer.

"She turned eighteen last week."

"I see," Garrett said, nodding her understanding. "Then you know that she's an adult."

The statement was far more than commiseration with an angry father, it was a statement of legally binding fact. Parents had control over their children's augmented reality up until their eighteenth birthday. They could require a son or daughter to share their theme throughout their childhood and teenage years. But once the child reached the legal age of adulthood, they were emancipated to choose any reality they wished. And clearly Jeb's daughter, the "harlot," no longer wished to be Amish.

The elder to whom Garrett had first spoken was growing more uneasy in direct contrast to, and possibly because of, her continued equanimity.

"Are you Keepers?" he asked, for the first time stepping out of character.

"No," Garrett said simply, knowing that her one-word response would only increase his unease by telling him exactly what he didn't want to know.

Keepers were a quasi-law enforcement agency that numbered in the hundreds of thousands. They could not see or control the augmented reality of others and had no more control over, or access to, the grid than anyone else. They were simply peacekeepers operating within the different themes, generally assigned to a particular theme much like a police officer would be assigned a particular beat. They dealt with the lower-level difficulties and crimes that had nothing to do with the grid itself. By admitting to the man that they were not Keepers, that left only one possibility for their identities.

The elder grew very pale. "We don't want any trouble," he said, his voice trembling slightly.

Jeb stepped forward, still belligerent. "Simon, I'm not going to stand by—"

Simon turned to him almost violently. "You will do as the council instructs you to do. You will do as I instruct you to do. And you will be censured for this most grievous violation of our ways."

It appeared that Simon's agitation finally communicated to Jeb exactly who stood in front of him. His eyes darted to Garrett, then went to the ground.

"I'm sorry, Simon. You're right."

Garrett examined Jeb at length, determining that his contrition, or at least his fear, was legitimate and that he would not cause further difficulty.

"Good," she said, "then we will be on our way."

The men all removed their hats, and the women, who had risen to their feet, curtsied as the three walked by. Garrett could hear their murmuring as they passed through the gated fence to an adjacent field, which drifted away as they put distance between them.

"I have never known anyone who could say so much with so few words," Mike said with approval.

"I'm not going to use words in situations where they won't do any good," Garrett replied, glancing at the small display that appeared in the palm of her hand, hovering just above the surface of her skin. "The border is about half a mile this way. Let's make certain 'Jezebel' left on her own accord."

Char stepped over the gnarled root of a tree. "This seems like something the Keepers could have handled, pretty mundane."

"Yes," Garrett agreed. She had already received a private communique explaining the reasoning. "They sent us out because they're re-evaluating the isolation permit, and technically this was a violation of the terms of the Amish agreement."

"Are you going to revoke their permit?" Mike asked.

"No," Garrett replied. "This is pretty minor stuff. Had we received any resistance, I might have considered it, but I think 'Simon' has 'Jeb' under control."

"That still doesn't explain why they sent YOU out," Char said, and Garrett smiled.

"I've given up trying to decipher the reasoning of the Council. Sometimes I think they do it just to keep me from getting rusty."

They were approaching the border, which was not visible in any way beyond the marking on the display. They crossed the grid-line, which was completely uneventful. Everything looked and felt exactly the same.

"Okay, switching AR to Sector 52-2."

And then everything changed. Before, they had been standing in a pastoral scene of rolling hills and babbling brooks. Now they were standing in a post-apocalyptic wasteland. The world was a junkyard of twisted metal and jumbled concrete. The gently flowing stream was now a toxic morass.

"Now this is more like it," Char said, examining herself. She was dressed in leather and chains, her full breasts pushed upward in a corset adorned with spikes. Garrett glanced down at herself. She was female once more, and dressed slightly more conservatively in leather pants, a vest, and some type of duster. She, too, bristled with spikes and chains, and apparently now she wore an eye-patch. Sometimes the engineers had quite a sense of humor.

"Now that's what I'm talking about," Mike said, glancing down. He was shirtless, his huge chest muscles bulging, tattoos on every inch of his dark skin. He was gazing down appreciatively at what looked like a metal athletic cup worn on the outside of his leather pants.

"I don't know," Garrett said dubiously, "that might be all cod piece."

"I assure you that's my package," he said with satisfaction.

Char snorted. "We might want to re-seed this noise generator as well."

They continued on and it wasn't long before they came across the first group of raiders. They were dressed as outlandishly as the Guardians, and Garrett felt like they were all fugitives from some bad movie from her childhood. This group outdid them in terms of piercings, however, which ranged in appearance from the mildly uncomfortable to the unbearably painful. One woman had chains running from her pierced lip down to the piercing of each nipple, which then disappeared down into the top of her low-cut pants, where presumably it was connected to something else that was pierced. She followed Garrett's gaze.

"Want to see where that chain goes, darling?"

"No thank you," Garrett said politely. "We're looking for a girl that came over the border last week, should be a new addition to your tribe."

The pierced woman shoved away from the pock-marked wall. "You ain't some of those Amish fucks, are you?"

Mike chuckled. "I assure you we are not."

She appraised him through slit eyes. "Ray! Get out here! We got some more of those Amish bastards out here!"

Ray and a whole group of his buddies came out, all of them as stupid as the pierced woman. They tried to appear menacing, dismissing Mike and leering at Char. They surrounded the three threateningly, obviously forgetting that they were merely living inside a theme. It was not uncommon, especially for groups who chose to live in extreme versions of reality for long, uninterrupted periods of time. This group clearly thought they were some type of hardened gang of criminals, an illusion Garrett was not about to allow to continue.

"That's enough," she said sharply, and snapped her fingers.

The effect was immediate and staggering. A blue flash of light flickered across the landscape, rippling outward, appearing almost to be an imperfection in the scenery, an EMF wave that bent and distorted everything it touched as it propagated.

Mike chuckled a low chuckle. He looked over to Char. "I never get tired of that."

The response of the raiders was more pronounced.

"Jesus fucking Christ, they're Guardians."

Ray suddenly remembered that when he was not leader of Satan's Riders, he was a mediocre accountant at a mid-sized law firm.

"Look, look! We were only kidding! What do you want? You can have anything!" He shoved the pierced woman towards them in panicked confusion. "Anything!"

Garrett felt as if she were dealing with a child. "Where is the girl who came across the grid-line last week?"

A young woman wearing leather pants, leather boots, a red head scarf, and a sheer, sleeveless cropped T-shirt stepped forward. "I'm Eliza, I mean Liz."

Garret looked upon her impassively. "Are you here of your own volition?"

"Yes," the young woman said firmly, then a little less confidently. "I think so."

Garrett tilted her head to one side. "Eliza?" she said, using the Amish version of her name. "Is anyone coercing you to stay?"

"No," Eliza said, shaking her head, then firm once more. "No, not at all. I've just had doubts. And I miss my family."

"We're your family now, babe," Ray said less than convincingly.

Garrett stepped forward and held out her hand, palm up. Eliza placed her hand on the palm, face down. A flash of light appeared between the two palms, and the data transfer was complete.

"That is my holograph contact, and I can be reached at all hours. You have the legal right to return to Sector 46-G-52-1 at any time, although upon your return, you will be bound by the customs of that isolation sector. Do you understand?"

"Yes," Eliza responded.

"Good," Garrett said, "And the rest of you?"

The response was muttered, anxious, and unanimously affirmative.

"Yeah, yeah, we got it."

"Good, I don't want to be out here again anytime soon."

The ride back to the station was uneventful and Garrett was left to contemplate once more why she had been sent on such a seemingly low-level mission. She wondered which council the order had come from. There were an endless number of councils, The Council for Education and Development, The Council for Order, Law, and Regulation, The Council for Wellness and Adjustment, all of which had darker functions that would have made Orwell proud of those names. But there were really only two that mattered, two that stood above all others, and only two that Garrett answered to.

The first was SCAR. SCAR had twenty members, five Master techno-psychiatrists, five Master Guardians, and ten engineers. The whole field of techno-social psychology had blossomed out of early experiments with social networking, then flourished when augmented reality took hold. Techno-psychiatrists researched and attempted to predict the mental and emotional effects of technology implementation. What the psychiatrists could predict, the engineers could create, and the Guardians could control. The Master Guardians were on SCAR to maintain the integrity and consistency of the illusion of AR. The rest of the council was staffed by the Master Engineers, five from the software side and five from the hardware side, each specializing in some facet of the creation and manifestation of the grid. Granted, there were millions of positions below them all fulfilling some role, from the intern, real-time texture mapper to the senior software automation engineer, but these twenty people stood above all with tremendous responsibility and power. The world no longer had presidents or kings or queens, but, SCAR, also known as The Supreme Council of Augmented Reality, ruled everything by pursuing the simple goal of maintaining a perfect, personal illusion for each person on the planet.

But there was one council above SCAR, one far more shadowy and exclusive, one known only as Echelon. It had only three members, two men and one woman who not even most members of SCAR had met face-to-face. And for some reason she could not pinpoint, Garrett was almost certain the order had come from these three.

CHAPTER 3

THE KEEPER GLANCED TO THE figure coming down the road, then did a double-take. He elbowed his partner in the ribs none-too-gently to rouse him from his inattentive state. His partner grumbled and stood upright, also turning his gaze to the woman coming toward them.

"Yeah, yeah, I see her. I don't know why you think she's so special."

The first Keeper tried not to stare at the approaching woman, thereby emphasizing his interest by his exaggerated disinterest.

"You've seen her locker, where she keeps her jumpsuit."

"So what, a couple of these weirdos have private changing rooms."

"No, I'm not talking about her room, I'm talking about the locker."

The partner eyed his friend. "You're not supposed to be in those rooms."

"I wasn't in there. I mean, not really. I caught her in the hallway as she was coming out, tried to get her talking so I could get a peek. Fucking creeped me out, though. She has this way of looking at you, like she sees right through you."

The partner snorted. "Everyone has that look."

"No," the Keeper said, shaking his head. "It was different. I don't know how to explain it. But it was different."

"You think she's a senior Keeper?"

The Keeper stared at the woman darkly. "I think she's a Guardian."

The partner exploded in harsh laughter. "Why the fuck would a Guardian live in an off-grid hell-hole like Refuge? Yeah, that's where I would live if I had almost infinite power, someplace where I couldn't use it."

That made too much sense to the Keeper, deflating him somewhat. "I'm just saying, there's something about her."

Garrett was near enough the two that they quieted. Of course her armor augmented her hearing so she had heard every word they said. And it was humorous to her for several reasons, but mostly because she was making no attempt to hide her distinctive black-and-gray uniform and had either Keeper chosen to go off the grid for even a moment it would have instantly confirmed her identity as a Guardian. But neither did so, perhaps because they did not wish to, or more likely, because it did not occur to them. The Keeper sentry would rather engage in amateurish subterfuge, attempting to peek over her shoulder at her locker rather than look at what was right before him.

"Hi guys," Garrett said mildly, then pushed into the gatehouse.

The interior of the gatehouse was simple. The primary space was a public changing room. Almost all public spaces, even those once segregated by sex such as restrooms, were co-ed. Since no one was actually seeing what you really looked like and crime was almost non-existent, the need for privacy had diminished. Anyone could imagine you naked at any time, so what use was it? The gatehouse was slightly different, however, because the public lockers were framed with small cubicles that could be shielded with a curtain pulled across the front. The reason for this small nod to modesty was that the gatehouse was one of the few places on earth that people removed their AR jumpsuits, which was a requirement to enter into Refuge.

There were a few residents of Refuge that Garrett recognized, and she nodded to them. They nodded back, watching curiously as she disappeared through the back door as she always did. She moved down the dimly lit hallway, stopped in front of an imposing looking metal door, then pressed her palm to the biometric scanner. The door slid smoothly open and Garrett stepped inside a small, clean, metallic room. The door slid closed behind her.

The protection on the door was minimal because it did not really matter if someone broke into the room. It was the locker in front of her, the one in which she would store her armor, that was protected beyond measure. It required eight unique biometric signatures from her, produced in an exact order that was randomly changed each day. The order was communicated to her by a series of flashing colored lights associated with each signature. The lights flashed, green, red, blue, yellow, orange, white, purple, then black, and then in order, she underwent a fingerprint scan, iris scan, voice analysis, face recognition, retinal scan, breath analysis, skin analysis for both DNA and scent, and finally a brain scan.

"Welcome home, Zen 12."

"Thank you," Garrett said as her locker opened, the sound of compressed gas escaping. True, she was speaking to an artificial intelligence, but that didn't mean she couldn't be polite.

Garrett began undressing. According to the engineers who designed her locker, seven of the eight biometric signals were unnecessary. The techno-psychiatrist who scanned her brain, who was also a neurologist, determined that her brain signature was so unique in the general population it was not only unlikely to be duplicated, it was unlikely it could even be reproduced by other than pure chance.

She pulled on jeans, a black T-shirt, some black sneakers, and a dark green jacket. Unlike most people walking into the gatehouse, she walked out looking exactly the same except for a change of clothes.

The few people in front of her walked through the scanners without incident while the Keepers looked on. Refuge was a designated "AR free" zone, and although not completely off the grid, the invasiveness of AR, as most residents termed it, was not ever-present. The scanners would identify any bit of technology that would overlay AR on Refuge or its residents.

Refuge had a small stable population and a smaller sub-population that fluctuated in a predictable pattern. There were always new residents who thought they were through with the grid, that they wanted "reality" in all its harsh beauty, but they generally lasted about a week. That hearty frontier spirit wilted under the banality of day-to-day life without the grid, and it was far easier to scratch that itch by joining the Oklahoma Trail sector where there was more excitement and the risk was purely theoretical. It reminded Garrett of the beginning of the 21st century, when military video games were ubiquitous, but military enlistment was at an all-time low.

Garrett passed through the scanners, as always, without incident. She nodded to the Keepers at the gate then stepped into Refuge. Most newcomers were disappointed because nothing looked that different from the world they had just stepped from. To their eyes, Refuge looked like any other run-down town, signs of dirt, disrepair, and disorganization evident everywhere. The city sign even had the "g" scratched out and replaced so that people were greeted with "Welcome to Refuse."

To Garrett's eyes, nothing looked the same. In the early days of robotics, there was a great deal of research testing human's acceptance of artificial life forms. Researchers found that people felt more affinity towards robots the more human-like they became. But there was this space where the robot was almost human, but not quite, where suddenly the humans were revolted, repulsed by the close-but-yet-so-far likeness. This space was called the Uncanny Valley and its study exploded when the field of AR began to grow.

But the Uncanny Valley had swallowed the world, and humans were so deep inside that valley they could no longer see over the cliff walls in any direction, and the valley had become so wide that for all practical purposes, it had ceased to exist.

But not for Garrett. Her eyes could discern between the dust that collected in the corners and cracks of Refuge, and the dust patterns the grid generated from a fractal or turbulence model with random noise levels. She could tell the difference between the rough, scarred wood of the "Refuse" sign and a carefully designed texture map with vector displacement applied. She could tell the difference between skin that was truly kissed by the sun and that which merely had a very good sub-surface scatter shader applied.

Refuge, although not completely removed from the grid, was largely what it appeared to be, as much as anything was before AR draped its veil over the world. All of the logistical functions, electricity, water, trash reuse/destruction, sewage conversion, were still part of the public system. The residents, like everyone on the planet, had the corneal implants. They carried the nano-particulates that nestled in the meninges of the brain, silently communicating with the grid and carrying massive amounts of data back to the Department of Statistical Analysis.

Although almost everyone was familiar with the corneal implants, few knew of the nano-particulates, tiny dust motes of an individual's cloned brain cells, 3D-printed into sensors that acted as transducers between the brain and the world around it, installed at the same time as the corneal implants. The sensors converted physical sensation to electrical signal, and vice versa, contributing monumentally to the illusion of the grid. Initially, the AR overlay had been merely visual, but the disconnect with the other senses shattered the illusion. But once smell, taste, and hearing were added into the mix, the illusion was almost flawless. Only touch remained out of the grasp of the engineers, the somatosensory system having too many inputs, not merely skin, but bones, organs, and muscles. It was Garrett's understanding they were closing in on this holy grail of artifice, however, by creating nano-particulates out of spinal material that would float in spinal fluid, intercepting whatever signals were transmitted from the various inputs and translating them into something "appropriate." Garrett had observed one experiment in which a blind-folded test subject placed her hand into a box and was asked to describe what she was holding. She was quite certain it was a soft blanket, perhaps lambskin or something similar, and the engineers all nodded to one another quite pleased. They did not reveal to the woman she was fondling a cactus.

Garrett reached out and ran her hand along the worn sign, enjoying its rough surface and the gentle squeak of the hinges as it swung on its rusty chains.

"Hey Garrett!"

She turned at the greeting and waved to her neighbor, Bill. Bill was a thin, lanky man, his arms and legs a little too long, his nose a little too large, his thinning hair rumpled, and his smile bright enough to light up a room.

"You coming to the Duck tonight?"

"Yeah," Garrett said, "probably."

"You know Rachel will ask me first thing," Bill said.

"Tell her I'll be there around 2000," Garrett said, reaching her doorstep. She unlocked her front door with an ancient device referred to as a key. When she had first moved to Refuge and purchased her small house, she had replaced the electronic door lock with the archaic mechanical device. Her neighbors had never seen such a thing. She allowed free examination of the magical equipment, and they marveled at its simplicity, the ease with which it worked. And finally one man, Daniel, stated the obvious.

"That thing is off the grid."

"Well," Garrett said, "as much as anything can be. But yes. It doesn't use any electricity. It doesn't talk to me, or open when I wave my hand, or set the thermostat in my house. But, I turn the key, and it unlocks, pretty much every time."

Within days, Daniel, a big bear of a man who liked to build things with his hands, had begun fashioning locks for everyone in Refuge. It became such a tourist attraction that they placed a mock door just outside the gates so that the curious could examine the item without having to actually leave the grid themselves, and without disturbing the inhabitants of Refuge.

The door opened with another mild squeal of hinges and Garrett stepped into her house. It was clean, but a bit disorganized, not cluttered, just comfortably unkempt. It had a holographic entertainment center in the front room where one could play games, watch movies, read, or any combination of the above in three dimensions. Although movies had gone through an experimental phase of audience interactivity, that had morphed into something very different. Originally, producers thought the audience wished to determine the twists and turns of the plot, the outcome of the story, but that was too much work and required too much thought and not what the audience wanted at all. Instead, movies had become much more like video games, in which the viewer could wander around and explore the room in which the actors were playing out their scenes. Or they could join in the action, fighting the enemy at parts until the more sedate parts resumed. Or at any time, they could touch anything in the scene and be linked to some bit of information that would satisfy their curiosity. It had changed the entertainment industry drastically because artistic camera angles no longer mattered. Rather it was the detail of the scenes and the degree of interaction that were preeminent.

Garrett rarely used the holographic system at all, mainly because it seemed very much like living within the grid and not that entertaining. It reminded her of people who used to play simulation games in which they held jobs, bought houses, got married, raised children, fed pets, in short, everything they did in real life. It all seemed very odd to her, something of a duplication of effort.

The house had a very simple layout: the front room, a bedroom, a small kitchen, and a small bathroom. It was a little over 500 square units, which in her childhood would have been considered tiny but now was considered spacious. Few people, even in Refuge, lived alone.

The green jacket was hung from a hook on the wall and Garrett settled into the adaptive memory foam couch. It shifted itself to her desired firmness and she relaxed, allowing her eyes to close. She did not sit in some painful lotus position, but merely kept her back straight and both feet on the floor, her hands comfortably resting on her thighs. She shifted her attention to her breathing, her focus on the gentle in-and-out of breath, the slow rise-and-fall of her diaphragm. The black nothingness that was not nothing but rather "no thing," full of emptiness, floated before her eyes, then expanded outward, encompassing everything. Fragments of thought drifted in, but she did not push them away nor did she grab onto them. Rather she let them fade away without giving them attention. After a while, the thoughts ceased and there was only the dark light of her mind, utterly still and utterly peaceful.

The senior director of the Department of Statistical Analysis stood before a wall of holographic displays that shifted continuously providing information from a system that processed 300 yottabytes per second through quantum relays. Most of the sub-systems were monitored by artificial intelligence, and the AI sifted through the binary signals that existed in the either/or state, or sometimes both, representing emotions, thoughts, sensations, sight, sound, taste, really anything that the human brain processed. The flashes of light signified everything from hunger to satiety, sadness to despair, mild pleasure to violent death, although the last was now extremely rare.

Very few of the systems were monitored by humans, and only one by the senior director of the DSA. This particular system monitored the feedback and status of the Zen Guardians, possibly the most important individuals on the planet. Zen Guardians were not born; they were created, groomed almost from birth. Chosen from the highest DNA stock, they were strong, healthy, intelligent, but more importantly, possessed balance, reason, and critical thinking. They also possessed an undefinable quality, a tolerance for ambiguity and a nonchalance that was almost psychopathic had it any other focus than the preservation of the grid. A Zen Guardian had to be capable of making the right decision at the right time in the right context, knowing that an hour later, that same decision in a different context could be completely wrong and even immoral.

The selection and identification of Zen Guardians was still something of a crap shoot. Although early attempts at genetic engineering had proved promising, humans learned the hard lesson that accelerating evolution was not a good idea. Bending natural selection to the whims of society had fairly horrific consequences as nature rarely gave something without taking something else away. When nature's take-away occurred over a hundred thousand years, it was not so noticeable. But when it occurred in a single life-span, or even in a single year, the consequences were far more evident. When one gene was modified, it was not a simple cause-and-effect relationship. That one gene might suppress another, which accelerated the growth of a third, which then mutated a fourth, which worked in tandem with a fifth, and so on. And even that complex scenario ignored the epigenetic ramifications. It was almost impossible to predict the outcome, and humans were reminded that the reason why evolution was so effective is that what did not adapt, died.

So Zen Guardians could not be created in that sense, but they were chosen almost from birth. And from those chosen, only a minute fraction would actually become Guardians.

The senior director looked up. A red light was flashing frantically, and the alarm, although muted, communicated the severity of incident. The director looked to the engineer monitoring the sensor display in question, but neither appeared anxious or even surprised.

"It's Zen 12."

"Very well," the director said calmly, "silence the alarm."

The director watched the red light blink silently. This was an almost daily occurrence, and sometimes more than once a day. The brain waves of Zen 12 settled into such an abnormal state that it triggered the alarm on a routine basis. The pattern was deeper than sleep yet stronger than major excitation, then fell into something resembling death. He had never met Zen 12, but he was told that the first time this had occurred, a major response team had been dispatched only to discover her sitting quietly, unharmed and awake. The scientists had wanted to take her away for research purposes, but the Intermediary had intervened and shut that down immediately. That did not stop Echelon from issuing a quiet edict that all of Zen 12's activity was to be recorded and forwarded to R&D for research. The director did not know if Zen 12 was aware of this edict.

CHAPTER 4

GARRETT WANDERED DOWN THE ROAD to the Rusty Duck, greeting several residents as she passed. The Duck was a sturdy, rectangular structure that appeared a little run-down due to the rough wooden shake siding that was askew in areas, the shingles collecting dirt and grime in their crevices. The planks of the wooden boardwalk flexed and creaked pleasantly as Garrett stepped on them, and the bells on the door jingled as she pushed through the entrance.

"Garrett!"

A buxom red-head was wiping down the bar, her full breasts threatening to spill out of a low-cut top as she worked the rag across the gleaming surface. Rows of bottles with exotic colored liquids reflected light on the mirrored shelves behind her. Her green eyes twinkled with bawdy humor and the mouth that was a touch too wide stretched into a grin. Although true accents were exceedingly rare anymore, somehow Rachel had managed to maintain a slight Irish lilt to her voice.

"Bill said you were coming. Duke will be so happy to see you!"

"Is he downstairs?" Garrett asked.

"You know that he is."

"I'll be right back."

There was a doorway to the right of the bar, one guarded by a very large man leaning against the wall with his arms crossed over his chest. His round face and babyish features contrasted with his stern expression. Above him over the doorway was a hand-painted sign that said in bright red letters, "By Permission of the Management," then in smaller letters "Refuge Residents Only."

"Hey Dan," Garrett said, greeting the large man.

"Hey Garrett," Dan said, "Go on down. Duke's in rare form tonight."

Garrett pushed through the curtains in the doorway and started down the stairs. The basement was dimly lit but her corneal implants adjusted instantly to the lighting. Once at the bottom, she glanced about the room, her disinterest pronounced given the scene before her.

Two women were naked and intertwined, engaged in acrobatic sexual maneuvers that entertained the small crowd around them. Further into the room, a man was chained, his member painfully erect as he was lightly beaten by a woman in high heels and a leather corset. Near the far wall, a huge bear of a man was mounting a woman on all fours, ramming her rhythmically from behind. Several other couplings were sprinkled about the room.

In one sense, it was all standard fare, decidedly unimaginative in a world where almost anything and everything was available for visual consumption. But little details stood out that made the scene strangely compelling. The lack of perfection in the women's features, the little pockets of cellulite visible on legs, faded stretch marks, the hairiness and slight layer of fat about the man's stomach that jiggled with every thrust. The basement of the Rusty Duck was a down and dirty, nasty sex club, one that provided a raw experience that many felt that no AR could match. It was that uncontrolled rawness that so affected the participants, increased the sexual intensity, and brought satisfaction despite the flaws and imperfections.

It affected Garrett not at all. "Hey Duke!" she called out across the room to the bear of the man.

Duke paused in mid-thrust, grinning from ear-to-ear. "Hey Garrett!" he called out, "glad to see you!"

He then resumed his thrusting as if uninterrupted.

Several other participants also paused in the midst of what they were doing to wave greetings to Garrett, which she returned. Then, without a backward glance, she went back upstairs.

"Here you go," Rachel said, setting a glass of sake down. "Nothing synthetic for you, this is the real deal."

"Thank you," Garrett said, taking a seat then taking a small sip of the warm rice wine.

Rachel dried the glass in her hands, then set it beneath the counter in front of her. "I'm sure Duke was happy to see you. I swear, he gets hard every time he even thinks about you."

This might have been a curious admission in Garrett's old life, but monogamy was not as desirable in this new world. Many cultural mores had simply drifted away. All infants, male and female, were placed on permanent birth control so accidental procreation was impossible. It was astonishing the number of problems this solved. To conceive a child, both parents had to make a conscious decision to have their reproductive capability activated, petition the Council for Wellness and Development to make it so, then successfully pass the required training. No one was ever refused. That had been one of the early concessions in the program to placate the right-to-lifers who had lost considerable political power and credibility when forced to face the devastating impact of extreme overpopulation.

Garrett took another sip of the wine. "He looked happy enough. Are you going to join him later?"

"Yeah," Rachel said, "Deena's coming in at 2300, then I'll head downstairs. Maybe you can go down and wave to him right before, get him ready for me again."

Garrett simply smiled, a gentle smile without judgment and it reminded Rachel why she so dearly loved this woman. Garrett was an enigma, one who shared little about herself. The residents of Refuge knew she had a demanding job, for she was coming and going at all hours, but she never appeared stressed, merely more thoughtful at times. And she had a subtle sense of power about her, one that might have been frightening were it not for that subtlety. And Rachel could not quite put her finger on it, but she had the feeling that Garrett was far older than she appeared, which would not have been odd except no augmentation was allowed in Refuge.

Rachel examined Garrett, making no attempt to disguise her admiration. Garrett was good-looking, not beautiful, but possibly more attractive because of that deficiency. She had warm greenish-brown eyes, sandy brown hair, an imperfect nose that seemed perfect on her face, pronounced cheekbones that were perhaps a bit too sharp, and a beautiful mouth with a strong cupid's bow. Duke often talked of that mouth when Garrett was not around, many times when he was burying himself in his wife.

A man sat down one seat over from Garrett at the bar. Daniel gave him a once-over, an assessment that indicated he would not be allowed downstairs. The man's clothing was new and ill-fitting, not because it was improperly sized, but because he was so very uncomfortable in it. Perspiration beaded on his brow even though it was comfortably cool in the bar.

"I'll have what she's having," he said, waving in the general direction of Garrett's glass.

"Are you sure, darling? Most people can't afford what she's drinking. It's not synth."

The man blanched, unwilling to spend a month's salary on a drink, but equally unwilling to admit he couldn't afford it.

"Put in on my bill, Rachel," Garrett said.

Rachel poured out a glass and set it before him on the bar. "Thanks," he said uncertainly. It was a very generous act, but he did not think this woman was hitting on him. He took a sip and his features flushed with heat from the liquor.

"How long are you in town for?" Rachel asked knowingly.

"Is it that obvious?" the man said, almost relieved his outsider status was revealed.

Garrett glanced over at him. It was more than obvious. Everything about him, his clothing, his mannerisms, his discomfort, revealed his non-resident status. But more than anything, he looked like he had a tic as he repeatedly glanced up and to the right, even jerking his head slightly in accompaniment to the eye movement. It was a dead give-away.

In the early days of the grid, controls had been built into the wrist area of the AR suits. But after the corneal implants, a more seamless experience was desired. Technology was developed to allow mental control of the basic grid functions: changing or adjusting the theme, altering appearance, changing parameters, etc. In theory, thought alone was sufficient to perform this function, but the majority of people were unable do so. So as an adjunct training method, young people were taught physical movements to accompany their thought commands. Borrowing cues from neurolinguistics, young people were trained to access different parts of their brain by looking in that direction. To connect to the grid, right-handed individuals were taught to look up and to the right, left-handed up and to the left, accessing the dominant hemisphere for visualization.

In normal circumstances, the movement was nearly unnoticeable. Right now, the man at the bar looked like he was having a mild seizure as he unconsciously tried to reconnect to the grid.

"How long have you been offline?" Garrett asked quietly.

"About two hours," the man admitted. "It's not really what I expected."

Garrett nodded. "You should probably finish your drink and head home."

"I agree," the man said, then downed the sake in one drink.

"Do you want a nanocapsule to go?" Rachel asked. The capsule was filled with enzymes that would drastically lower his blood alcohol and sober the man instantly if need be. It was a technology built into the AR suits, but he wasn't wearing his suit right now.

The man started to take the capsule, then changed his mind. "Seems a shame to waste such good wine," he said, "and my suit's in the changing room at the edge of the sector, er, town."

"All righty then," Rachel said breezily, "on your way now."

The occupants of the bar watched the man leave with varying expressions. Daniel looked scornful, Rachel appeared entertained, and Garrett simply watched him go. She stood up.

"I should head off as well."

"So soon?" Rachel cried. "Ah, work, as usual."

It was a mild probe, an unsuccessful quest for information, but Rachel never stopped trying. Garrett extended her hand, palm down, over the bar, and a light scanned her handprint. A holographic receipt briefly appeared, then dissolved.

"Good night, Rachel. See you later, Daniel."

Garrett went to bed early and slept soundly for several hours. She was awakened by the quiet hum that notified her that a transmission was incoming. It was a high priority message and did not require her acceptance, so the warning was purely an act of courtesy. It was an extremely short courtesy, however, as the holograph appeared above her midsection in the bed. The image of the woman flickered, then stabilized, then solidified to vivid three-dimensional form. It was life-size, from the waist up, and since Garrett was lying on her back, it appeared almost as if the woman was straddling her.

The woman did not speak at first, merely examined the prone figure over which she hovered. Garrett waited patiently beneath the inspection.

"You have been summoned," the holograph said at last.

"By the Council?" Garrett inquired.

"No," the Intermediary said, "by me."

"Very well," Garrett said calmly, "I will leave now."

The building housing Echelon, REACH, was one of the most protected on the planet, although many wondered why this was necessary. Sabotage was almost impossible as AI ran most of the systems and the human factor had largely been removed. Engineers were carefully screened in their youth for psychological factors that would make them unsuitable for their positions. Those who were unsuitable were subtly "redirected" to other vocations. The Engineers who had access to critical systems were constantly monitored. Vital signs and voice patterns were measured to detect any abnormality that might indicate deception, anxiety, or stress. Brainwave patterns were analyzed and compared, both against the general population and against an individual's norm. It was difficult to plot against a machine that could read your mind. The system had multiple redundancies built in, and it was self-perpetuating as it learned and learned.

But really, what kept the vast majority of the population in check was a profound apathy, an apathy built on the illusion of meaningful activity, fostered by imaginary goals and achievements that stimulated the human brain in exactly the same way as had they been real. And that was what made AR work: the unmindful brain did not differentiate.

Garrett passed through the enormous arch that was the entryway into the building. The archway scanned her, getting an instantaneous read-out of her identity and state of mind. It knew if she was permitted to enter and if she was expected. It analyzed the totality of her biometrics and determined she was not a threat.

"Welcome back, Zen 12," came the soothing female voice.

"Thank you," Garrett said.

To Garrett's knowledge, the members of Echelon never left this building. If they met with SCAR, it was by holograph in VR, and that was rare. Most functions inside the building were performed by machines. Few ever came before Echelon in person, and Garrett guessed she was summoned more frequently than the next thirty visitors combined.

Each of the three members of Echelon had elaborate suites connected to the Assembly Room, and each of the three suites had an outer forum that was only slightly less imposing than the Assembly Room. Garrett entered the forum in the center. The room was dimly lit, illuminated only by the walkway lights and the various electronic sensors embedded in the walls and high-vaulted ceiling. There was an elevated platform and desk reminiscent of a judge's bench in the archaic legal system. And upon this bench sat the Intermediary, dressed in a series of robes that suggested she had risen from bed for the meeting.

Garrett stood by the seat on the small platform below the dais.

"You may sit down."

Garrett sat down, both feet flat on the floor, her arms settling onto the armrests. The Intermediary examined the posture: open, comfortable, and confident.

A light to Garrett's left attracted her attention and she turned to the holographic screen slightly behind her. It was an analysis of her brainwaves overlaid with the feedback from the nano-particulates. She glanced to her left, where another holographic screen displayed a compilation of various vital signs. Although the Intermediary could have viewed the information on her own visual plane, she had chosen to make them visible, meaning she wanted Garrett to know she was being monitored. However, the holographic images were positioned where Garrett could not see them, but where the Intermediary could watch them as she watched Garrett, as was her custom.

"Do you mind?" the Intermediary asked.

"Of course not."

The Intermediary was a cold, elegant woman. She was beautiful in a mechanical sort of way. Perhaps it was her lack of expression that gave rise to the machine-like comparison, or perhaps the deliberation in her speech. Perhaps it was the voice itself that, although not monotone, never rose or fell very far. Perhaps it was the content of that speech, which could be brutally incisive while politely devastating, not deficient in tact but dispensing with it when unnecessary, which in her view, was almost always.

"I wish to continue our interview."

"Very well," Garrett said.

The Intermediary examined the monitors, noting that internally and externally the equanimity of the response was the same. "I want you to tell me more of your life before the experiment that cured your cancer."

This was a common subject in the Intermediary's questioning, one probed at length over the months and years the "interview" had continued.

"Do you wish to know something specific?"

"Tell me of a milestone, an epiphany if you will, in the development of your mind."

Garrett sat quietly for a moment, thoughtful. The Intermediary watched the screens. As always, there were no signs of deception, suppression, or concealment. No distress. No anxiety. Little if any emotion, just thought.

"I remember when I was very young, probably less than four years old, of being able to contemplate infinity. It was a wonderful experience, being able to think as far into the future as possible, then pushing just past that. It is difficult to describe, almost a feeling of mental ecstasy that I enjoyed repeatedly."

"And what happened to that feeling?"

"I slowly lost the ability, and could no longer reproduce it. I remember standing in front of a mirror and having the sensation that I was losing something, that something was slipping away from me. Again, I could not have been more than four years old."

"And you mourned the loss of this ability."

"Greatly," Garrett admitted, "for many years."

"Can you reproduce it now?"

"I cannot."

"This saddens you."

"It does," Garrett said calmly. But then a small smile tugged at the corner of her mouth. "But at least I was there for the moment I lost my Original Face."

The Intermediary was familiar with this phraseology. Zen 12 had been found in solitude in a Buddhist monastery and that spiritual practice permeated every facet of her being. Although few religions were given any credence by the secularists, they were intrigued by the mental discipline required of Buddhism. Substantial research confirmed the benefits of meditation on focus, intelligence, critical thinking, and physical and emotional well-being. Although direct stimulation of the brain had proved fruitful, it was not as effective as meditation. It was incorporated into the training of the Engineers and Zen Guardians, and even encouraged on a voluntary basis for the Keepers.

But there was no one quite like Zen 12.

"Tell me of your teenage years. You had an epiphany then, as well."

"I did."

"Describe that for me again."

Garrett's eyes stared straight ahead, unfocused, something that always intrigued the Intermediary. According to the neurolinguistic school of techno-psychiatry, most people would look to the left and slightly upward when trying to remember something. Zen 12, however, always looked forward, an action more associated with absorbing sensory information, usually visual.

"I was thirteen," Garrett began. "And it was a very simple moment. I was lying in bed daydreaming, my mind somewhere else as it always was. Pretending I was someone else, somewhere else, doing and being other things. Living with another family. Having a different life. I was dreaming of being rich, of being in a mansion, lying in my bed." Garrett trailed off.

"Go on."

"Suddenly I realized that, as I was lying there, on my bed, eyes closed, nothing would change. Regardless of what surrounded me, lying there with my eyes closed, everything would be exactly the same. What I was thinking, what I was feeling, were completely independent of what surrounded me. The fiction of being wealthy affected me just as powerfully as the reality would. It is hard to express what an enormously powerful realization this was."

"But you feel you misinterpreted this realization."

"I did. It unmoored me from reality, and I spent years in a fantasy world, because the fantasy world was just as satisfying, if not more so, than the real one. I overlaid my own reality on the world long before the grid."

The Intermediary silently watched the various holographic monitors, several more which had activated behind Zen 12.

"And when did this understanding change?"

"Life has a way of intruding upon fantasy. Or at least it did until the grid. The fantasies became less satisfying, more difficult to maintain. I began meditating, off-and-on at first, then with more consistency. My mind became increasingly unaffected by external events, not through suppression or denial or control, but simply because things, if given no weight or attention, passed right through me. That was where I truly began to understand the experience I had perverted. I had sought to satisfy myself with unreality because it affected me the same. In truth, the ability for events to affect me was arbitrary."

Garrett was silent for a long moment and the Intermediary watched the holographs.

"In the texts I read, there was a phrase repeated over and over. 'Like a snowflake on a hot stove.' It was used in many contexts and seemed to refer to a state of being that I didn't understand. One night, I was deeply grieving the loss of a pet, experiencing all sorts of regret and guilt, fairly torturing myself with bitter self-accusation. I decided to try and meditate, although I didn't think it would help. I began counting my breaths and quieting my mind, letting the chaos settle. I could still feel the grief in my chest like a knot, like a weight that made it hard to breathe."

The Intermediary's own chest rose and fell in the tomb-like silence of the room.

"And then the sorrow was just gone," Garrett said, "it wasn't suppressed or avoided, it was just gone. Disappeared. And the sensation was so startling, it jarred me and the grief came rushing back. I wasn't sure what had happened, so I again settled into meditation, and again, within minutes, the grief simply disappeared. And it was only then that I understood that emptiness that contains everything, understood that nothing else can exist there. It is not through rejection, or avoidance, or even active detachment, there's just nothing there, and it melts away like a snowflake on a hot stove."

"And yet you do not consider yourself enlightened."

"I am not."

"You saw the results of the experiments with the Engineers," the Intermediary said, slightly changing the subject. "Their meditations have yielded great success. Measurable improvement in mental focus, emotional control, stress tolerance. Several consider themselves to have reached enlightenment."

Garrett was silent, but it was evident the Intermediary was waiting for a response.

"They have not," she said quietly.

"How can you be so sure?" the Intermediary said, looking for any signs of bias or jealousy, anything that would weaken such an unequivocal opinion. As always, there were none, not in the monitors, not in Zen 12's face.

"Because they seek it."

There was a rare flash of anger in the Intermediary's eyes. "Your words frustrate me."

"That's not my intent," Garrett said, "it's just that words are inadequate to describe something that must be experienced."

The drumming of the Intermediary's fingers on the surface before her was loud in the room. Of the few who had seen her in person or even in holograph, this was a dangerous sign, one that usually resulted in flight from her presence, whether physical or virtual.

But Garrett simply sat there.

"You know," the Intermediary said, "when you passed the Advanced Turing test, SCAR voted almost unanimously to have you retrained."

"Retrained" was one of those words that had taken on a far more ominous meaning with time. Garrett's "retraining" would likely have resulted in the deactivation of most of her hippocampus. Or she could have been imprisoned, constantly subjected to experiments to get at the source of the unique ability measured in the Advanced Turing test: the capability to identify augmented reality with 100% accuracy 100% of the time.

"I know," Garrett said, then after a pause. "Why did you stop them?"

The drumming ceased, the hands moved to the lap where the fingers interlaced. It was a bold question, indeed, the very act of posing a question to the Intermediary was bold. "I have my reasons."

For a moment, only the mild hum of the electronic sensors could be heard, then the subject changed once more in a calculated manner. "The sex club, the one in the basement in Refuge."

"Yes?"

"Does it excite you?"

"No."

"Why not?"

Garrett knew her answer would be deeply dissatisfying to the Intermediary, possibly even angering her further.

"There is no 'why' there. It simply does not."

"But you can still experience sexual pleasure."

"Yes," Garrett said evenly. "What I lack is desire."

"What is the difference?" the Intermediary asked bitingly.

"Pleasure is a physical sensation; desire is the longing or craving for that sensation. One is in the here-and-now, the other takes one away from the present."

The Intermediary's demeanor changed abruptly, and Garrett knew the interview was over. Her dismissal, however, was also a summons.

"The Council wishes to see you in the morning."

It was a test, for Garrett was always being tested. The decree meant that she did not have time to go home and sleep, that her too few hours of rest were at an end.

"Very well," Garrett said, and stood up.

"You are dismissed," the Intermediary said. Garrett bowed slightly and left the room.

The holographic display before the Intermediary shifted and then expanded to fill the room. She watched as Zen 12 walked through the outer forum, then on to the lobby, curious to see her actions. Most would have made use of the sleep cubicles that were pervasive in the city, but Zen 12 did not exit the building. Instead, she sat down on a bench that adjusted to her slender frame, then closed her eyes.

The Intermediary watched her, and somewhere off in the Department of Statistical Analysis, a red light began flashing until the Senior Director silenced the alarm.

At 0755 hours, a gentle vibration, a haptic warning from her armor, alerted Garrett she was due to meet with Echelon at 0800 hours. She rose, stretched her neck and legs, then entered the outer forum she had so recently vacated. This was the formal meeting place for the Council of Echelon, although few ever attended their meetings in person. The Council Members would sit on the upper platform, either in person or in holograph, at the enormous circular table that doubled as an information kiosk. The glass surface of the table shifted with data and statistics, casting light upward in a manner that many felt gave the council members a distinctly sinister look. The curved walls also served this purpose, so that the room could be awash in statistical feedback. It was all an illusion of course, for the walls and table were actually quite plain. But the grid overlaid whatever information the members of Echelon currently chose to view. And the manifestation of the grid in the building was highly controlled: once a person passed through the arched gateway, all individual control over AR ceased. In this building, you saw what Echelon wished you to see.

Whatever matter had brought Garrett here today was important, for the members of Echelon were all present in the flesh. She took her place on the small platform beneath the circular table.

"You may be seated," the Intermediary said.

The Intermediary sat in the center, now clothed in the formal robes of the Echelon Council, a stark contrast to her earlier casual wear in her personal forum. The man to her left was thin with sharp features, pale skin, thin lips and thinning hair. This was Sanction, and although the duties of the members of Echelon were legion, each primary area of responsibility could be gleaned from their names. The man to her right was Arbiter, heavy-set with dark, swarthy features, hooded eyelids, and the pugnacious jawline of Mussolini. Although few beyond Garrett would have been able to detect it, this was in fact how the Council appeared regardless of AR.

Garrett sat quietly while the three Council Members examined her.

"There has been an incident."

The Intermediary's words hung in the air, understated in a manner that only magnified their import. There had been nothing on the communication lattice, no tactical alerts, no bulletins or broadcasts.

"What kind of incident?" Garrett asked.

"There has been a murder."

Garrett parsed these five words, more for what was unsaid than said.

Violence was carefully coordinated. Those who desired it could interact in a virtual manner, where interaction was consensual and pain and injury was monitored. The effect of the violence was also measured, to ensure that it was cathartic and not escalatory. But true crime was almost nonexistent, partially because the environmental factors leading to criminal behavior had been removed. Poverty did not exist. Abuse of children was prohibited. Education was free and required. Socialization was handled by the state, regardless of theme.

Additionally, those who had low activity in their anterior cingulate cortex were closely monitored. This area of the brain, responsible for regulating behavior and impulses, was remarkably apt at predicting true aggression. There was an algorithm for treating such a deficiency. If it was level 1, the deviant was simply encouraged to express their violent behavior in themes where there were no consequences. The grid was amoral; it valued only efficiency. Even the term "deviant" did not connote judgment, rather was used in the sense of statistical deviance, as in deviance from the mean.

If the deficiency, was level 2, the deviant would be required to undergo retraining, in which their ACC would be directly stimulated to attempt to bring the activity level closer to the norm. If the deficiency was level 3, and the deviant was immune to retraining and correction, they would be eliminated. Again, the system valued only efficiency.

Spontaneous violence could not always be predicted, however, and other parts of the brain were carefully monitored. There was a specific combination of signals from the amygdala, limbic system, and thalamus, coupled with the release of cortisol and adrenalin, that indicated behavior was spiraling out of control. The AR suits could inject a series of drugs and hormones that would counteract the flood of rage, immobilizing the perpetrators if necessary.

Murder, needless to say, was extremely rare, and rather than a personal crime was considered something worse: a flaw in the system.

"I see." Garrett said.

Sanction smiled his thin smile. Zen 12's response was as understated as always.

"Where did the murder occur?" Garrett asked.

"Sector 64-M-22-8," the Intermediary said.

Garrett mentally accessed the sector. "Not an isolation sector per se, but the dominant theme is shared by 72% of the local population. A medieval fantasy world."

"Yes," Sanction said, a trace of sarcasm in his high-pitched voice, "Dungeons and Dragons."

"What does the Archive say?" Garrett asked.

The "Archive" was the active record of everything. It was compiled and distilled by DSA and included brainwaves, biofeedback, biochemical fluctuations, physical location, etc. of humans within the grid. It also included high-quality feeds from the corneal implants kept in quantum holographic storage arrays. Like so many other projects, the Archive had started as a "customer service" application, providing feedback on the status and success of the grid. Now it recorded everything, and its uses went far beyond customer service.

"There is no record, at least not for the suspect."

The room fell into complete silence as Garrett contemplated this impossibility. Both Sanction and Arbiter glanced over to the data displayed in front of the Intermediary. It was her custom to monitor Zen 12's reactions, and she was doing so now. But the bio-diagnostics barely registered above baseline. There was no fear or surprise, no anger or disbelief, no significant emotional reaction at all. Just indicators of deep thought.

"You will go to Sector 64-M-22-8 without delay to investigate this matter."

"Very well. Do you wish me to conduct the investigation alone?"

"Do you trust the discretion of your co-workers?"

Arbiter glanced to the Intermediary. It was a fascinating question. It meant that, despite the volumes of information collected on Zen 64 and 82, despite their constant monitoring from birth, despite the never-ending surveillance and evaluation of their performance, the Intermediary still gave weight to the opinion of Zen 12.

"I do."

"Then they will accompany you."

"Very well."

"Obviously you understand the magnitude of this assignment. Do you have any questions?"

"I do not."

"Then you are dismissed."

Garrett stood up, bowed slightly to the council, then left.

"Are we sure that she is even human?" the Arbiter said with a trace of mockery.

"I assure you that she is," the Intermediary said.

Something in her voice caused both men to glance over at the coldly beautiful woman, then to one another. Arbiter fingered the display on the table.

"If you gentlemen will excuse me."

The Intermediary disappeared back into her quarters. Arbiter and Sanction simply sat there.

"Zen 12 was here again last night," the Arbiter said under his voice. Members of the Echelon Council were not monitored, so in theory his thoughts, speech, and vital signs were private. But like most who spend their lives destroying the privacy of others, he suffered from paranoia, a sense of never quite being safe.

"I know," Sanction replied.

Although usually scrupulous in the caution of his speech, Arbiter could not help himself. "Do you think it's true? What is said about them?"

"I don't know," Sanction said curtly, "and it is unwise to speak of such things."

Sanction left through the door to his personal forum, and Arbiter was left at the table alone. He retreated to his own quarters, if for no other reason than to escape a nagging feeling of exposure.

CHAPTER 5

THE CABIN OF THE AIRCRAFT was of a comfortable, minimalist design. The cushioned chairs folded down into beds. The central desk doubled as a dining table. The small shower recycled all water. A small kitchen area provided liquid and solid sustenance made to a desired look and taste, although without AR, the food was very bland. Hyper-sonic flight was a rarity and was most often used by Guardians as there were so few of them to deal with an enormous area of responsibility. The flight itself was rarely noticed any more since technology eliminated the sonic booms of previous incarnations. Most never even saw the plane, although in certain sectors, the starship Enterprise was occasionally sighted, and in others, the Millennium Falcon.

"I still don't understand how this happened," Mike said. "The Archive records everything. There should be a blow-by-blow description of what went down."

"I checked in with my handler at SCAR," Char said, "he said the Engineers are still trying to trace the glitch."

Glitch, Garrett thought to herself. That was the logical conclusion. A mistake rather than a conscious act. Not the murder, that was without question a conscious, intentional act. It was the concealment of the act, the obfuscation, that concerned SCAR far more than the fact that there was a person dead.

"We should review the record from the victim's point of view," Garret said. She tilted her head slightly to address the computer. "Play back timeline from Sector 64-M-22-8."

The holographic image sprang to life in the center of the table. The AR overlay was active, and the room appeared to be the interior of a rough hut, or an unfinished room. The walls and floor were wood. The light was dim, coming from a few candles and the fire that glowed warmly in the hearth. A kettle was suspended over that fire, and because its contents were an illusion, Garrett could smell the stew even in the reproduction. It was a simple, rustic dwelling.

The room was seen from the peripheral vision of the victim. It seemed to be a young woman based on the unblemished appearance of the hands in her lap. She wore a flowing medieval gown and sat in a chair before the fire. She hummed to herself as she knitted a wavy, rope-like pattern on something that might have been a scarf.

People of the dark ages would have been astounded that people in the future would choose to occupy their world, although arguably, without the famine, filth, and pestilence, it wasn't so bad.

A door could be heard opening in the background, but the young woman didn't stir.

"You're home late," she called out.

There was no reply, so the woman continued humming as she knitted. She paused for some reason, perhaps sensing a presence behind her, and started to turn her head. The visual plane shifted violently, then the view turned in a nonsensical direction, winding up at an odd angle in a pool of spreading red liquid. The only thing visible was a crumpled body clothed in a medieval gown, one now missing a head.

"Whoa," Mike said.

The AR deactivated, but the corneal implants continued to record. Little of the room could be seen, but the floor was no longer rough-hewn wood, but a smooth silicon-based polymer surface. The body was no longer clothed in a medieval gown but in a gray AR jumpsuit. The blood stain on the floor was the same, however, a thick pool of red that slowly spread out from the now-unseeing eyes.

Garrett quietly contemplated the scene, then tilted her head. "Play back timeline without AR."

The scene repeated from the young woman's point-of-view. The room was far more plain, a non-descript heating element where the hearth was, a food dispenser where the kettle had been, a simple AR jumpsuit instead of the flowing folds of the gown. The hands were feminine and a little more weathered, but the young woman had altered her age by only five or six years. Interestingly, the scarf did not change. The materials were real, as was the skill of the knitting.

"You're home late."

The voice was essentially the same, unmodified, again indicating she had not altered her age by much. The ensuing violence was also much the same, a wrenching change in perspective, a slight bounce from the floor, then the nausea-inducing roll as lifeless eyes settled on their own corpse.

The three Guardians were silent for a moment.

"So I'm guessing that SCAR is more worried about the lack of feed from the suspect than the actual murder," Char said.

"Right," Garrett replied. The murder would have been unfortunate, a failure of the predictive model in the system, merely something to be analyzed and learned from. She addressed the ceiling. "Where are the nearest public feeds to this incident?"

"There are six publicly monitored areas within an 800-meter radius. Eleven within a 1600-meter radius."

That was thin coverage, Garrett thought.

Even in a super-surveillance society, there were trade-offs. In Garrett's youth, cameras had begun to proliferate, blanketing such cities as London and New York. No one could walk down the street without being recorded. Cellular phones that used GPS to orient themselves began to track people, doubling down on identifying where you were at any given time. The implementation of RFID tags, which were embedded into everything, closed that gap even further. Satellite imagery ensured you could be located precisely almost anywhere.

Warfare and disaster destroyed much of that infrastructure, but it had been reborn and reimagined with the grid. The grid self-monitored through a dazzling array of sensors, providing constant feedback on its current state. In terms of power, the hardware no longer had the linear structure of the old electrical grid, but rather was designed in a looped structure to prevent the domino-like failures of the past. It was capable of absorbing excess current while sending the appropriate amount down the line. And most importantly, sections were isolated from one another, so that even if one sub-sector went down, it would not affect adjacent sectors. The adjacent sectors could act as an instantaneous backup to the failed area.

So the power to implement AR was always present, as was the surveillance that came with it. But public cameras had become rare. The corneal implants and the nano-particulates were fail-safe tracking methods, eliminating the need for exterior cameras. The corneal implants provided a constant visual record, and research had established that it could take as few as three people sufficiently triangulated to recreate any scene. Because most people now congregated in densely packed areas, detailed three-dimensional recreation was generally effortless.

And that was the trade-off: despite a constant source of power and surveillance, where there were no people, there might not be a visual record. Many larger public spaces were still recorded with exterior cameras, but that was a porous net compared to the blanket provided by the corneal implants.

Garrett rubbed her lower lip with her index finger. "Somehow this suspect was able to deactivate their feed." She looked away from Char and Mike, addressing the computer. "Within the first 800-meter radius, cross-reference all available feeds with the visual record from the exterior cameras. Is there anyone present who is not emitting a feed?"

This daunting computational task was handled within seconds.

"Negative. All visible figures have associated feeds."

"Expand the query to the 1600-meter radius, same parameters."

This took slightly longer.

"Negative. All visible figures are accounted for in the public areas."

"So, he switched his feed right back on after the murder?" Char proposed.

This should have been impossible from a technological standpoint, but the hypothesis made sense. "We don't know that we're dealing with a 'he,' but statistically that is the overwhelming probability," Garrett said. She raised her chin. "Beginning at the crime scene, begin triangulation of all feeds in an outward expanding radius to the 800-meter mark. Identify any figures seen in one or more feeds that do not themselves have a corresponding feed."

The Zen Guardians waited while the computational tracking was complete.

"There are no such incidents."

"How can that be possible?" Mike said.

Garrett tapped her chin. "The hallway outside the victim's location, do you have any associated feeds immediately following the incident?"

"There is a single feed available approximately 36.4 seconds from the incident."

"That's close," Char said hopefully.

"Real-time spatial reconstruction is impossible from the single feed," the computer continued. "Would you like the view augmented with historical feeds to provide three dimensional feedback?"

In situations where something was observed by only a single person, details could be filled in with cross-references from other recent feeds, for example, someone who had walked down the same hallway minutes or even hours before.

"No," Garret said, "first show us the single POV."

The Point-of-View was much like the feed from the victim. A first-person perspective of someone walking down the dimly lit corridor. This person was also in "Dungeons and Dragons," and the hallway looked as if it belonged in a boarding tavern as candles flickered in the alcoves. Down the passage there was a large, oval mirror on one wall with elaborate gilded filigree around its edge. There were several decorative shields hanging on the opposite wall. The hallway was empty and the walk was completely uneventful. The person walking saw nothing and did not react in any way, but turned into his own domicile a few doors before that of the victim's.

"Replay with AR deactivated," Garrett ordered.

This replay did not add anything substantial; it was merely a plainer version of the first.

"Replay with feed augmentation."

This was a more interesting replay as the scene sprang into three-dimensional life. Ghostly figures moved with purpose through the recreation, sometimes walking through one another. While the primary feed was viewed at full opacity, the historical feeds faded in proportion to their distance in time. Some figures were so ephemeral they seemed to float down the hall. It was a strangely beautiful and compelling recreation, given additional poignancy when the soon-to-be murdered girl, a real ghost, transparently glided down the hallway to her doom.

"Nothing," Mike said. "How can this guy walk around and not be seen?"

"We know the suspect is not being recorded," Garrett said, "we don't know about being seen."

"But that couldn't go on very long, being seen but not recorded," Char pointed out. "The grid will flag anomalies, and if this guy interacted with another person, chances are it would begin to throw exceptions."

That was true, Garrett mused. The grid self-monitored its internal consistency to maintain a uniform illusion. It was not 100% fool-proof, but if a "non-object" was exerting influence, the grid would want to know what it was. "So the suspect is not being recorded, and may or may not be seen. And somehow their absence goes unnoticed by the grid."

"No one jumps on and off the grid, not even us," Char said.

That was also true, Garrett thought. Although she had enormous power over the manifestation of the grid, she could not separate from it any more than anyone else could. Even in Refuge, without AR, the grid was omnipresent. Every person was tied to it at birth, and separated from it only by death. And as evident by the playback of the victim, sometimes even death wasn't sufficient.

"This is no glitch," Garrett said with growing certainty. "This is some-one with extraordinary technical knowledge." She thought her next query through carefully, then addressed the computer by name.

"Hybrid, begin cross-referencing all data sources in a 3200-meter ra-dius from the crime scene. Use all corneal feeds, scanners, public transpor-tation, AR suit biofeedback, everything available. Identify any incidents where there is a break in continuity of a feed, where a person seems to suddenly appear or disappear. Use a time period four hours before and four hours after the murder."

Char and Mike had exchanged glances when Garrett addressed the computer by name. Hardly anyone did that anymore, and Garrett only did it when she was deep in serious thought. Unlike most names, Hybrid was not an acronym but rather a description of the quantum analog/digital monolith that helped regulate the grid.

"So we have a suspect with extraordinary technical knowledge," Char pondered aloud while Hybrid thought, "one capable of jumping on and off the grid."

"And one capable of disguising that fact," Mike added.

"And one capable of regulating, altering, or removing bio-feedback to the grid," Garret said.

"I hadn't thought of that," Mike said. "A murderer capable of cutting off someone's head must have been showing all sorts of biomarker spikes leading up to the crime."

"Yet the system noticed nothing," Garrett said. "Another technological feat. This was premeditated, well-planned, and flawlessly executed. But why?"

Char addressed Hybrid. "Give us a run-down on the victim."

A full-sized holographic image appeared of the woman. She was dressed in the standard AR jumpsuit, of medium build, average height, plain features, perhaps dead-center of the distribution curve that was the human race. She was unremarkable save for the gentle smile that seemed to illuminate her otherwise simple face.

"Show most recent AR version," Garrett ordered.

The image shifted. The woman was thinner, taller, younger, more beautiful, now dead-center of the considerably more narrow distribution curve of how the human race chose to perceive itself. She wore a flowing, silken green gown, the large cuffs of the sleeves decorated with elaborate stitchery. She still possessed the gentle smile, however, as AR did not generally alter expressions.

"Occupation?" Garrett asked.

"She is a virtual seamstress," the computer replied, "she designs many of the period costumes for various medieval themes."

A flow of lighted text and images appeared in front of the holograph, and each of the Guardians was free to sort through what interested them.

"A claimed standard Christian affiliation," Mike said.

"Married for seven years," Char commented, "husband accounted for at the time of the crime. He was informed of the death, although not its manner, and was suitably grieved. No children."

"No recent recorded altercations, disputes, or biofeedback spikes," Garrett said, "or in fact, ever. Acceptable work performance, no financial or health issues. Lives in the medieval theme 85% of the time." Garrett looked up slightly. "Do you seen anything unusual about the victim?"

"The subject is unremarkable," Hybrid responded. "There are no variables associated with a higher probability of victimhood."

"Is it possible she was a random victim?" Char asked.

"It is possible," Garrett said, "but the planning was so perfect."

"Maybe it was geographical," Mike suggested, "maybe he was just looking to kill someone in that building. Maybe just someone in that room since it was so close to his exit."

"Then it comes down to why," Garrett said. "Maybe not why her, but why murder at all."

All of this was dissatisfying to Garrett, but instead of continuing to ruminate on it, she took a deep breath and let it go. To grasp too tightly to anything at this stage would introduce bias, perhaps eliminate as-yet-identified options.

"The earlier query returned no results," Hybrid intoned.

That did not surprise Garrett. No one had appeared or disappeared from the grid within 3200 meters of the murder within an 8-hour window. She thought about expanding the time frame, but intuition told her that would be fruitless.

A slight change in the cabin pressure indicated they had arrived at their destination. The touch-down had been so smooth it went unnoticed.

"Well," Garrett said, "let's go blend in with the locals."

"Shift to dominant local theme."

Garrett issued the command, but the effect was the same for all three. The bland, industrial interior of the hangar changed to an enormous cave. The smooth gray tiling transitioned to a dirt floor littered with rocks and the bones of animals, one that appeared to be a unicorn. The artificial lighting disappeared and was now replaced with warm, flickering light from the torches burning at equal intervals along the wall. Garrett glanced back at the plane and saw that the engineers had solved the problem of the modern conveyance with their usual sense of humor.

"I see we flew here on a dragon."

Mike glanced back and gave a little stutter step away. "Damn," he said.

The creature was enormous, sleeping soundly, the belly scales scraping against the rocks with every breath. Every exhalation was accompanied by a whiff of sulfur.

"Let's hope that none of the locals get it in their head to embark on a quest to kill our plane," Garrett said. She examined her companions. "You," she said, addressing Mike, "are obviously a black knight."

"Hey now," Mike said jokingly, then looked down at his ebony armor. "Oh, I see what you're saying." He accessed his current profile. "Yes, I am a level 66 knight. The level cap for this theme is 100, but there are only a handful at my level or higher."

Char, too accessed her profile. "I am some sort of rogue character, proficient with a bow and arrow and daggers. Oh crap," she said, lifting her hand to her ears and fingering their shape. "And I'm an elf."

Mike snickered.

"She's a level 67 elf," Garrett pointed out, and it was Char's turn to laugh.

"And I'm a wizard or sorceress or something," Garrett mused, glancing at her clothing. The robes were elaborately embroidered with glyphs and symbols that were probably significant. She had long dark hair and her skin was very pale. The looks on her companion's faces caused her to activate self- reflection mode. She sighed at her appearance.

"I wonder what this is all about?"

"Mmm," Char said.

"Wow," Mike said.

Garrett did not care enough to access her full profile, and would do so only if needed. But for whatever reason, this role demanded she be exceptionally beautiful, at the extreme edge of what the engineer statisticians would allow. She pulled her hood over her head.

"Let's go."

They made their way from the cave and exited out onto a bustling medieval square. A butcher was selling gigantic cuts of meat of mysterious origin. A blacksmith was hammering a sword, sweat on her brow and her muscles bunching with the strain of swinging the titanic hammer. Various vendors were hawking wares, blankets, trinkets, vegetables, and the like. Briefly, Garrett switched the grid off, an act that would have caused anyone else to stumble and most to trip and fall. But her gait did not change as the world changed dramatically, becoming sterile and banal: the butcher was selling nothing more than a processed vegan soy product, the blacksmith was a tiny girl swinging a ballpein hammer, and the trinkets, blankets, and vegetables were far less esoteric than they seemed.

To the right were a few ComRes buildings, a living solution that had become far more popular than home ownership. Much like the dormitories of old, they provided small apartments for people, but differed from an apartment in that the kitchen and recreational areas were communal. The techno-psychiatrists theorized that this type of living had become more desirable after the loss of over 90% of the human population. Everyone had lost someone, and some had lost everyone; now no one wanted to be alone. The development of certain "themes" played a large part in the formation and evolution of the individual ComRes.

To the left was a stack of bunking cubicles, much like the five-by-five stack on the main path to Refuge. Many now chose to forego personal dwellings entirely and had only a bunking cubicle to sleep in. Some tubes were just large enough to crawl into. Some were slightly larger and had just enough room for a bed, a small holographic projector for entertainment and communication, and a relief tube. Community restrooms were available, as well as community kitchens. How and where one lived was dependent on choice, but also on how much one contributed to society. Some chose to do very little, happy in their illusion, and they were cared for on a minimal level, living in the cubicle bunks.

Garrett switched the grid back on. The cubicle bunks looked like wooden cots, or perhaps tented bunk beds, in this reality. The ComRes buildings were wooden huts with thatched roofs. The communal dining area was a tavern, and the communal restrooms were a row of outhouses, which to Garrett's mind probably should have been a ditch for historical accuracy, but the outhouse was an acceptable solution.

They came to the physical location of the crime scene and looked up.

"The Rose and Crown Inn," Mike read aloud. "I'm guessing this is the place."

The rough-hewn door swung open with a creak and slight resistance, and many in the place sized up the newcomers. The first floor was a pub of sorts with long wooden tables and benches, a few smaller tables with chairs, and a bar adjacent to the far wall with rows of casks behind it. Dwarfs, elves, humans, half-orcs, gnomes, occupied the tables, all wearing the gear that specified the classes of warrior, rogue, cleric, wizard, and some that were frankly indecipherable to Garrett. Some had a number flickering above their heads, one that indicated their level, although the display was optional and only the more advanced chose to activate it. Char and Mike outranked everyone in the room with the exception of a level 70 warrior in the corner, but that was not evident because their displays were not turned on.

Garrett nodded to those gazing curiously, moving through the throng with that quiet confidence that Mike so admired. They made their way to the uneven steps that led to the second floor. The barkeep started to warn them that the second floor was closed due to maintenance repairs, some malfunction of the grid, but then refrained. Something about the demeanor of the three, especially that "mage," made him think they would not be coming back down anytime soon. If they were what he thought they were, that malfunction must have been pretty bad.

A formidable looking mercenary clothed in leather armor stood blocking the stairs. He was a senior Keeper, tasked with maintaining the integrity of the scene. None of the Keepers knew what had occurred on the floor. The original Keeper who had responded had already been "retrained" and now remembered nothing. The senior Keeper present was not aware of this, but he knew that whatever happened was serious because he was not normally dispatched to routine work, and the other Keepers assigned were nearly as senior as he.

"Greetings, Keeper," Garrett said, lowering her hood. "Where is the Guardian assigned to this sector?"

"She was here late last night, but should return shortly."

"Very well," Garrett said, "we're going to look at the area."

"Of course," the Keeper said, nodding respectfully. He flashed a look of warning down to the other Keepers, a notice to look sharp. He wasn't exactly sure who these three were, but all Guardians were imposing as hell, and these three more so than usual.

The hallway looked much as it had in the virtual reconstruction, easily identifiable as the same location. Garrett examined the wooden walls, the flickering candles, the hanging shields, the mirror, and oriented herself. She stood in the middle of the hallway, tilted her head and looked to the left.

"Play back previously requested feed augmentation."

The virtual recreation sprang to life once more and the hallway was populated with the ghostly figures. A half-orc walked right through Garrett, greeting a ghost elf as they passed one another. The passing was fortuitous in timing because it recorded each occupant in great detail, allowing Garrett to analyze even their facial expressions. The future victim wafted down the hallway, humming to herself. The ebb and flow of characters revealed nothing out of the ordinary.

Garrett started to speak, then turned to the Keepers as a courtesy. "You may want to look away."

Both did with alacrity, and even the senior Keeper down the hallway turned his back on the scene. Although Garrett would not actually be deactivating the grid, she was going to show a recreation where it was not present, and even that was too jarring for most.

"Play back augmentation without AR."

The plainer version of the recreation replayed, and the same people, albeit with distinctly different appearances, moved through the hallway. The half-orc was a slender young man, the ghost elf was a heavy-set woman, and the victim was far less elegant in her gray jumpsuit than her lovely green gown. But still she hummed and walked down the hallway with a mindless, dreamy air. Again, nothing was unusual.

Normally, such a recreation, all events overlaid on top of one another, would be sufficient. All individuals present would have feeds. If no one was present, there would be no record. Without a feed, someone could walk down the hallway undetected at any time, in any one of the numerous gaps where no one else was present. A quick check revealed a significant gap within the quarter hour preceding the murder where the suspect could have slipped in unseen. When faced with the impossibility of someone removing themselves from the grid, the recreation was discontinuous and incomplete. It would serve no purpose to play it back sequentially.

"Play back post-incident feed augmentation, AR activated."

Specifying post-incident eliminated many of the ghostly images, but Garrett wanted the time frame narrowed further. She moved down the hallway. The Keepers had all distanced themselves when faced with the horror of going off the grid, but Garrett still spoke quietly.

"Play back first minute of post-incident feed with augmentation."

For 36 seconds, nothing happened. The hallway was empty. Then the man who had provided the first POV appeared at the top of the stairs. He was dressed as a bard in green tights and leather jerkin, carrying a lute over his shoulder. He meandered down the hall.

Garrett looked around her, at the walls, the mirror, the floor, the candles, the alcoves, looking for anything. She saw nothing, and the minstrel entered his room.

"Repeat playback with AR deactivated."

The sterile corridor appeared, and again, for 36 seconds nothing happened. Then the man, now dressed in a plain gray jumpsuit, appeared at the top of the stairs. The lute slung over his shoulder was much the same, although it was nondescript without the texture and displacement mapping that provided so much detail. He made his way down the hallway alone and disappeared through his door without event.

"Nothing," Char said in frustration, but Garrett was not frustrated. Something was here, she just could not see it yet.

"Let's go into the room."

The walls and floor were the familiar wood. The light from the few candles was still dim, and the artificial fire glowed much the same in the hearth. The kettle was still suspended over the fire and smelled of stew. It looked very normal, or at least very normal for a serene medieval hovel, and the illusion was complete until one noticed the severed head lying next to its own corpse. The body was clothed in the lovely green gown, a gown the eyes stared at lifelessly.

Garrett examined the body. The scarf the woman had been working on was on the ground near the feet. The pool of blood had dried and the weapon that had inflicted the mortal blow lay next to it. It was a distinctively curved, single-edged blade. The guard was square and the grip was long: a katana. Something fluttered to life in the back of Garrett's mind and she waited to see if it would spring into focus. It did not, and she did not grasp for it. She tilted her head to the side.

"Hybrid, perform Deep Forensic Analysis."

Light emanated out from Garrett's torso. It looked mystical, as if the glyphs and symbols on her robe were illuminated and pouring forth blue light. In reality, her AR jumpsuit was performing multiple scans, analyzing blood patterns, searching for fingerprints, looking for bodily fluids, measuring the core temperature of the body. It was measuring the murder weapon, calculating forces and angles of attack, matching the blade edge to the wounds to ensure mechanism of injury. It would examine all reflective surfaces in the room to see if any images would be captured in the victim's feed.

"Do you have sufficient information to approximate a simulation?"

"Affirmative."

The ghostly image was now seated in front of the hearth, knitting. A virtual door opened behind her and both Mike and Char looked to it as if it would reveal the suspect, then reminded themselves there was no information to fill in that part of the simulation.

"You're home late," the dead woman said.

The sword appeared behind the woman, floating in air, swung at the angle, velocity, and force that matched the injury pattern, blood spray, and position of rest of the head. The head separated, bounced to the floor, the body collapsed, the scarf fell, and the blood pooled. The sword was set down gently, not dropped, and the simulation stopped.

"Continue the simulation," Garrett ordered, and the simulation re-activated. Mike and Char looked at one another while Garrett carefully listened. Approximately 28 seconds later, the door closed and she turned to the other Guardians.

"I wanted to hear the door close. The suspect should have been in the hallway the same time as the bard next door." Garrett tilted her head and addressed empty space.

"What else was found in DFA?"

"Eight sets of fingerprints identified," Hybrid began. "One belonging to victim, one belonging to husband. Six belonging to others inhabiting this ComRes identified as friends or acquaintances. DNA corroboration to the same eight individuals."

"The six that do not live here," Garrett said, "they are all accounted for and have feeds at the time of the incidents?"

"That is affirmative."

Garrett turned to Zen 64. "Go interview them. See what you can find out."

"You got it boss."

She turned to Zen 82. "Go track down the bard from next door, ask him if he saw anything. Then interview the husband."

"I'm on it."

These interviews would have to be delicate, but Mike and Char were more than capable of circumnavigating the landmines this case presented. Simply asking someone "did you see anything?" would have to be rephrased since everything a person saw should already be in the Archive. Garrett turned back to the scene. The room had provided little new other than the sword. Everything matched up with the victim's feed. She had been attacked from behind. Decapitated with the katana. DFA provided an approximate size of the suspect given the arc of the sword and force required for the decapitation. The first Keeper had arrived within minutes, alerted by DSA of an unexpected fatality, and the suspect had already disappeared.

Garrett's eyes drifted back to the sword. The thought again tried to surface and she unfocused her eyes and concentrated on her breath to allow it room. Her eyes refocused.

"Hybrid, is the sword a replica?"

"Negative. It appears a genuine relic from the 17th century. It is in excellent condition."

"Can you trace its origins?"

"Negative."

Garrett carefully considered her query. "What period was this sword constructed in?"

"Based upon the age and style of the weapon, it is Shinto."

A continent away, the Intermediary sat watching the live feed from Garrett's corneal implants. It was fascinating to watch what the Guardian watched, to see what she saw, to see where her eyes lingered, to see where they lingered not at all. And to do so while watching her vital statistics, her brainwaves, was a most intriguing exercise. And as the brainwaves spiked into a pattern generally associated with a revelation, the Intermediary quietly drummed her fingers on the desk in front of her.

Garrett exited the crime scene and thought to take one last look at the hallway. She stood before the gilded mirror.

"Hybrid, what is this mirror in this theme?"

"This is the Mirror of Opposition. The proper command word will create a duplicate of anyone gazing at their reflection."

"Does it work?"

"It does. However, no one has yet discovered the command word."

Garrett started to move on, then stopped at the mirror once more.

"Hybrid, play back post-incident feed from single POV with as much 3D augmentation as possible."

The computer complied and Garrett watched the mirror carefully. Nothing happened. She started to leave to examine the stairwell when she stopped again, staring at the mirror intently. She slowly turned around to examine the shield hanging on the wall opposite.

"Play back post-incident feed again."

Garrett watched the shield with the same intense concentration, but again nothing happened. Her eyes followed some unseen path back to the mirror, and she examined the gilded edges of the decorative frame.

"Play back post-incident feed again."

Garrett mentally counted the seconds in her head. The door to the victim's home closed. The bard appeared at the stop of the stairs and began walking toward her. Very subtly, almost imperceptibly, the light changed on the gilded filigree.

"Stop."

The computer waited patiently as Garrett thought through her next few words. "What is the depth setting for Raytracing in this rendering?"

"Three."

That made sense. It was dimly lit, light wouldn't travel that far, it would not take much to fake minimal reflections without wasting processing power on unnecessary calculations. Light would bounce once, twice, and then a third time, but then that would be all.

"Hybrid, I want you to temporarily disable any alerts to DSA and reroute them directly to Echelon."

"Understood."

"The light pattern I am seeing on this edge of this mirror, identify the source."

"There is no source present, it is an anomaly," the computer said calmly, and the expected alarm was transmitted.

"Calculate an origination source in the shield across the hall."

"Done."

"Now reflect that image backward once more and recompile an origination source in the mirror."

"Done."

"Now play back the post-incident feed once more."

And so Garrett watched the mirror as the door up the hallway closed. The bard appeared at the top of the stairs, and as he appeared, a shadow on the floor appeared in the mirror, and whatever cast the shadow walked right by Garrett unseen. Garrett stared down the hallway at an imaginary retreating back of someone who had nearly left no trace.

"Analyze the shadow," Garrett said quietly, "see if you can develop any type of physical profile of the object that cast it."

"Understood."

After examining the back stairwell and the alleyway, Garrett pulled her hood over her head and returned to the lower floor of the ComRes. She found a small table in a corner and ordered a tankard of mead, paying for it with the paper script that appeared in her pocket. The mead was synthetic but of acceptable quality, and she sipped it quietly while she considered the situation. The stairwell and alley had provided nothing. There were no feeds close enough in time to identify other potential anomalies, and as the timeline forwarded and the area of search expanded, it became a futile task.

Garrett took another sip of the mead. Someone was capable of turning themselves invisible. Someone had walked down a hallway and not been seen or recorded by the grid, nor, according to Zen 82's update, been seen by another individual in the same hallway.

Garrett turned her attention to the people of the room. Everyone present was occupying the same medieval theme. A quick analysis of biomarkers and vital signs revealed nothing atypical, just revelry and mild intoxication. An acoustical analysis of their feeds indicated she could speak quietly in the corner and not be heard. The high-level warrior was still across the room and sent several challenging glances her way, but Garrett surmised his challenge was directed at her mage persona and not at her per se.

A slender elf wearing leather armor approached her table, the number 62 hovering above her head. The number seemed to get her great respect from the patrons of the tavern, but it was another number that Garrett addressed her by, one that would have terrified those present.

"Zen 125," Garrett said quietly.

The elf took the seat across from Garrett. She had been a Guardian for years, was well-respected within the agency, and ruled Sector 64-M-22-8 and its adjacent sectors with absolute authority. She could have acted as Queen of the Dungeons and Dragons theme, or even King if it suited her whim. As most Guardians, she chose to move unseen and unknown through the throngs, changing her appearance often, and attracting as little attention as possible. Her quiet competence had given her a favorable reputation within the Guardians, who favored expediency and effectiveness above all else.

But she could not hide the near-worship of the individual sitting across from her.

"Zen 12," she breathed out. "It's an honor to work with you."

"Thank you," Garrett said simply. "Do you have any new information?"

Zen 125 shook her head. "I've received your updates and those of Zen 64 and 82. I have nothing that you don't have, and your cross-referencing of all available feeds was new to me. It never occurred to me that someone might be capable of removing themselves from the grid."

"It's one possibility," Garrett said. "There are others."

"But it's the one that makes the most sense. Someone came up that back staircase, entered the woman's room, killed her, then went back down the same stairs. And the grid didn't see him, record him, or know that he was there."

"Nor did the man walking down the hallway," Garrett pointed out. "I'm just curious why the grid didn't notice this person's absence."

"Is it—," Zen 125 began hesitantly, then paused at the absurdity of her speculation before hurrying on. "Is it possible he was never on the grid?"

Statistically, this was a zero-probability event, but Garrett did not rule it out for those reasons.

"Whoever did this has extraordinary knowledge of the inner workings of the grid, and no one could gain that knowledge without being a part of it."

Zen 125 breathed a sigh of relief that Zen 12 gave the heretical thought little weight.

Char and Mike arrived in the tavern and joined them at the table. After greeting Zen 125, Mike shook his head.

"The interviews went quickly. None of them even know she's dead. One thought the disturbance on the second floor was the husband, that he had done something to the grid."

Tampering with the grid was a major offense, one possibly exceeding murder in terms of severity. "Why would they suspect him?" Garrett asked

Mike again shook his head. "Not genuine suspicion. The guy didn't come out and say it, but he didn't have to. He was interested in the victim and not above removing a rival. All petty stuff, nothing that pointed to the murder."

"The husband was clean, too," Char said. "He knows his wife his dead, but he thinks she had a heart attack. She had pulmonary issues and was fond of stimulants. According to him, she never went over the pre-scribed limit, but she lived at the maximum all the time."

Garrett was unsurprised, but would follow every lead.

"We will take the sword," Garrett said to Zen 125, "have it analyzed in an attempt to trace its origins."

"And you're sure it's not a replica?" the elf asked.

"Initial analysis shows it's from the 17th century, but a more in-depth analysis is warranted."

"Hard to believe something like that survived," Char murmured.

A flashing in the corner of Garrett's eye alerted her to a message. She addressed the three Guardians in front of her.

"I am being recalled. Please follow up with a DFA of the stairwell and alleyway." She nodded to Char and Mike. "I will meet with you when you return."

Garrett stood to excuse herself when a commotion attracted her at-tention. The level 70 warrior had grown boisterous and been joined with several companions, all with level 60 or higher designations flickering above their heads.

"Tiran has confirmed the presence of the dragon! We leave to do battle!"

A cheer went up in the tavern and Garrett motioned for Mike and Char to turn on their level indicators. The level 70 warrior paused as he saw two very powerful rivals appear in the company of the level 62 elf. The timing of their revelation could not have been coincidence.

Zen 125 watched the scene unfold with fascination. Zen Guardians could handle a situation any way they saw fit, but by far the most encouraged method was to remain within the theme, to avoid breaking the illusion if at all possible. From what she had heard, Zen 12 could snap her fingers and shut down the entire sector. Zen 125 wondered if she would use that power to keep the plane from being destroyed.

She didn't have to because the engineers had given her a different sort of power. She removed her cloak with a flourish, and many in the room gasped. She mentally flicked the display switch, and her level indicator illuminated above her head.

It was the number 100.

"Oh my god, it's Iggwilv."

Garrett took a brief moment to access her profile and learned that was indeed her name. "Iggwilv" was an evil, selfish sorceress with enormous power and a proclivity for sexual manipulation. Apparently she was the greatest villain this theme had ever known.

"The dragon is mine," she said coldly to the rapt room. "Any who even lay eyes upon it will meet with my wrath."

This was indeed a profound threat as Iggwilv was the only person in the kingdom who could actually reduce the level of another person, even down to level 1 if she chose, a fate worse than death.

"Forgive me, my Queen," the level 70 warrior said, and went to his knees.

"You are not forgiven," Iggwilv said contemptuously, "but I will let you be."

Many in the room groveled before her as Garrett turned and gave the slightest wink to Zen 125. She then exited with a stately, malevolent grace.

"Is it always like that working with her?" Zen 125 asked as the room returned to its abnormal normalcy.

"Oh yes," Mike said, laughing. "It's always an adventure."

"Who recalled her?" Zen 125 asked, uncertain if it was an inappropriate question.

"Probably one of the Councils. For whatever reason, they like to have her in person."

"One of..." Zen 125's words trailed off as the implication of the words sunk in. "She goes before Echelon?" the elf asked in disbelief. "In person?"

"Yes," Mike said. "From what I understand, she is the only one."

"You will give us your report."

Garrett stood before Echelon because she had not been told to take a seat. And even though her every move, thought, heartbeat, breath, and conversation had been monitored, she repeated the events and findings of her trip as they had unfolded in chronological order.

When she finished, Arbiter rubbed his chin.

"So you have no motive, no suspect, and no leads."

"Correct," Garrett said calmly.

The Intermediary tapped her lip with her fingertip. Sometimes it was important to query Zen 12 as carefully as Hybrid.

"If you were the murderer," Intermediary began, "and you were able to remove yourself from the grid. How would you disguise your absence?"

Garrett had spent a great deal of time thinking of nothing else on the flight back. Logically, the suspect had to be on the grid under normal circumstances. It was not possible to move through society for any distance or length of time without the anomaly being flagged. An alarm would be sounded in DSA. So the question was, how did DSA miss the absence?

"If I had the technological expertise involved in this crime, the ability to remove myself from the grid for even a short time, I would disguise my absence by making it appear as if I were asleep."

Sanction leaned forward in his seat as Garrett continued.

"Out of all of the states of being, that would be the easiest to fake. There is no visual record. There are few biomarkers, and they follow predictable patterns. A set of personal data could be collected, compiled, slightly randomized, and then substituted in place of a live feed. I would think several hours, possibly a full night, could be gained by such a tactic."

"But as you said," Sanction remarked, "that would require tremendous technological expertise."

An update came in and the Intermediary processed it. Garrett did not turn around to look at the holograph the Intermediary was examining.

"Your companions found nothing of note. In fact, were it not for your identification of the anomaly, the investigation would have revealed nothing that was not already known. What does the anomaly tell you?"

"The perpetrator has given a command to the grid so that their visibility is zero."

The Intermediary noted that Zen 12 continued to use the neutral pronoun, unwilling to settle on a male or female designation until provided proof.

"The grid, therefore is not recording their presence," Garrett continued. "Also, the suspect cannot be seen by anyone with AR activated."

"Then basically he is invisible," Sanction said sarcastically. "No one deactivates AR."

"No one except Guardians," Arbiter said. "Do you think he can be seen, in person, without AR activated?"

"That is unknown."

The Intermediary's fingers began tapping. "Was the anomaly a mistake?"

"That is one possibility," Garrett replied calmly, a calmness that Arbiter found extraordinary because even he grew uneasy when the Intermediary began her casual drumming. "But it is unlikely."

"Why?"

"The invisibility command was in effect for diffuse, specular, shadows, reflections, and refractions, yet it was disabled on a third-level bounce of light."

"Why?"

Garrett was silent for a long moment and the Intermediary's eyes flicked to the holographic displays behind her. Both Arbiter and Sanction leaned forward in their seats.

"I don't know."

"Why do you *think* it was disabled?" the Intermediary said, her tone that of one dealing with a child, even though Garrett's demeanor had not changed.

"It was a message," Garrett said at last.

"A message to whom?"

"To me."

Sanction was startled and leaned forward to ask why she thought the message was directed at her, but apparently the Intermediary already knew the answer.

"Like the sword?"

"Yes. Like the sword."

Sanction's eyes drifted to the Intermediary. There were times when it seemed the Councilor was nearly at war with Zen 12, a war Zen 12 refused to fight. Or perhaps it was not a war but a very prolonged chess game. Either way, the Intermediary always dealt with Zen 12 with an intense undercurrent that was present with no one else.

"You are dismissed for the moment."

Garrett nodded. She knew that meant she could not leave. This time she would take advantage of one of the sleep cubicles

The three members of Echelon watched the Guardian walk from the room.

"What is the significance of the sword?" Arbiter asked as soon as she was gone.

"Zen 12 is unique in many ways," the Intermediary said, "and she is the only Guardian who practices Shintoism."

"Shintoism?" Sanction said with thinly-veiled sarcasm. "She believes that rocks and trees are possessed of spirits?"

"Not exactly," the Intermediary said. "She does not practice it as a religion, but subtly adheres to a belief system in which even inanimate objects are imbued with a spiritual energy."

"And she passed the psychological screening with an admission of this fantasy?" Sanction replied, his sarcasm no longer veiled in any way.

"She is the most effective Guardian to have ever lived," the Intermediary reminded him. "And wields power that would have corrupted any other."

"That's true," Arbiter said grudgingly. "But who beyond this Council knows of her belief? Her records are deeply classified."

"That is another mystery."

It was always the same. She was on her back, her arms and feet restrained. She was naked save for a cloth draped over her torso. The light in her face was blinding, even behind closed eyelids. Sweat poured from her brow and she could taste blood in her mouth where she had bit her lip to keep from screaming. The pain in her arms was enormous, blocking out all sight and sound. She struggled against the restraints, hearing voices that sounded like they were underwater. They were concerned, shouting, there was the sound of running feet, something had gone terribly wrong...

Garrett sat up in bed, nearly striking her head on the low ceiling of the sleep cubicle. She was bathed in sweat and her AR suit compensated by cooling the thin pocket of air surrounding her body. Her breathing was harsh and uneven coming out of the dream, and she took several mindful breaths to calm it, rejecting the suit's suggestion of the administration of a sedative.

There was no courtesy warning as the Intermediary flickered to life in front of her. The woman examined her at length without greeting.

"You had the dream again," she said at last.

"Yes."

"I wish to see you in my chambers."

The sleeping cubicle Garrett occupied was just outside REACH, and it was but minutes before she was again passing through the great Arch that scanned and approved her entry. As usual, the hallways were empty and quiet save for the chronic thrumming of the building that sounded like the low volume heartbeat of a humming bird. The Assembly Room was also empty, unsurprising since the Intermediary had specified her chambers. However, the Intermediary's outer forum was also empty, leaving Garrett to stare at the door that remained. The lock clicked, indicating access was available, and Garrett slowly pushed through into the Intermediary's inner forum.

The room was much like the outer forum in that glass and metal were the predominate design materials. It was unlike the outer forum in that there were signs of actual comfort, a couch, some chairs, a large glass sculpture in which water ran continuously downward like a waterfall. There was even a bedroom at the far side of the spacious entryway in which a large bed could be seen. The sensors and holographic displays were ever-present, however, for the Intermediary never removed her finger from the pulse of the grid, just as she never removed it from Garrett.

"You will sit," the Intermediary said, and Garrett complied, seating herself across from the woman who was dressed more casually but somehow seemed more coldly formal for the change. The Intermediary examined Garrett, clasping her hands together and pressing her index fingertips to form a peak which she pressed to her lips.

"Are you angry with me?"

Garrett's thoughts had not yet returned to equanimity, although the readout behind her told the Intermediary they were already remarkably close.

"No." Garrett replied after a long silence. "You could not know the anesthesia would not work on me."

"And yet ten years later you still have nightmares of the event."

"Yes. I meditate on them."

Garrett could tell that her lack of anger displeased the Councilor. The Intermediary collapsed her peak and propped her chin up with one hand while the fingers of the other began their drumming.

"I assume you have analyzed everyone sleeping in the vicinity of the crime scene?"

The dramatic change of subject did not faze Garrett. "The analysis is on-going, but at this time, there are no leads."

"And if that yields no results?"

"I will have to consider other hypotheses."

"Such as?"

"That this individual is not on the grid at all."

"You told Zen 125 that you did not think that was possible."

"No. Zen 125 suggested that the suspect was never on the grid. I did not think that was possible. To gain the ability to remove oneself from the grid would require intimate knowledge of its inner workings. That would be impossible unless achieved from the inside."

"So you misled her."

"I told her as much as she needed to know. Her suggestion, properly phrased, was a good one."

"And yet I'm guessing you had already considered it, hence your ready response."

"Yes."

"So how does one remove one's self from the grid?"

"There is only one way anyone leaves the grid."

The Intermediary stared at her. "So we are searching for a dead man?"

"Or someone who has faked their death. That is done all the time in Sector 64-N-26-4."

"Yes, but without success."

"Perhaps someone has succeeded."

The Intermediary considered the possibility. "That still does not explain how this person is able to move about unknown and unseen. It is one thing to do so for a short period of time to commit a crime. It is another to live that way."

"That is true," Garrett agreed. "It would be impossible to remain in any inhabited area for any length of time undiscovered."

It went without saying that the uninhabited areas were uninhabited for a reason: nothing could survive in the irradiated zones.

"You said you thought this murder might have been a message to you," the Intermediary continued. "What kind of message?"

"I don't know," Garrett said. "Perhaps a warning, a display of power. Perhaps just an attempt to get my attention. But to what purpose, I don't know."

"Then there will be more incidents."

"Yes," Garrett said, "there will be more."

CHAPTER 6

"SHE'S DOING THAT THING AGAIN."

Char stared out the glass window of their office to the training area below. A quick glance around the quad showed that many in the building were doing the same thing, staring out their windows at the spectacle below.

Garrett was not doing anything spectacular, at least to her mind. She was simply working out, whether that meant running, applying eccentric and concentric pressure to her muscles with the various available machines, or beating the hell out of the martial arts simulator. What was different from the way others used the equipment was the fact that she used no augmentation at all: no stimulants, no steroids, no inhalants, no injections, and no exoskeleton.

"I tried that one day," Mike said, "and I lasted about five minutes."

"I watched one guy try it," Char commented, "and he was injured inside of three. I don't know how she does it. Just the potential for injury is nerve-racking."

"At least she's not training with her sword," Mike said. The whole building came to a stop to watch that spectacle.

Apparently Garrett finished because the heads in the windows disappeared as people went back to work. A short time later, Garrett appeared in uniform.

"Feel better?" Mike asked.

"I always do," Garrett replied.

"And how was your report to Echelon?" Char prompted.

"About the same as always."

Char was disappointed. She was enormously curious about Echelon, but Garrett was always circumspect.

"I have a new assignment," Garrett continued, "one I'm going to have to go on alone."

"That doesn't sound good," Mike said.

"I will be going into Sector 64-N-26-4."

Both Char and Mike stared at her in silence. It was Mike who finally spoke.

"A or B?"

"B."

"Echelon is sending you into the Matrix alone?"

"That's really the only way of going into the Matrix without being discovered."

"Yeah, but..." Mike said, his tone dubious.

"I know," Garrett said. "But it's not dangerous for me. The danger is in shattering the illusion, which I will avoid."

"We'll still be standing by for a retrieval, just in case," Char said firmly.

"Thank you," Garrett said simply. "I'm going home for some rest, then will head into the Sector this evening. I will call if I need you."

Sector 64-N-26-4 was a dark, dank, cyberpunk dream world. It was an isolation sector so everyone present was on the same theme. Gigantic, neon billboards lined the rooftops and broadcast an endless array of oddities for sale. The towering buildings blocked out much of the light even during the day. It rained almost every day of the year and the pavement was slick and black, reflecting the neon pinks and greens of the signs. The Sector was full of wannabe hackers and techies who utilized pre-written code to bring down mischief upon each other.

But it was still on the grid, and the hackers and techies were truly wannabes because anyone with any degree of skill had already been absorbed by DSA. It reminded Garrett of the early days of the internet where "N00b69" was a 16-year-old boy who could hack into a bank using some code that was freely available on the world wide web, when pa$$word was considered cutting edge security, when people had no idea the amount of control that was already being exerted on them by unseen servers controlled by unseen operatives in invisible government or corporate agencies.

Garrett found the New Rose Hotel and approached the check-in kiosk. She waved her credentials that identified her as a nobody, and was assigned a room. Her presence attracted only mild interest from the occupants lolling around the lobby having intense discussions about things that didn't matter.

Her room was spare: a sleeping area that was more bunk than bed, a small kitchenette, and a bathroom that had a toilet and a shower. Undoubtedly, with AR deactivated, the bed was a bunk, the kitchenette was a food dispenser, the toilet a relief tube, and the shower a hygiene cubicle. But Garrett did not deactivate AR. In fact, she was not even wearing her Guardian armor, but rather was clothed in the simple gray jumpsuit that everyone else wore, and right now, the jumpsuit made it look like she was wearing a pair of jeans and a T-shirt with a faded Star Wars logo on the front of it. The classics still had a great deal of respect in this noir world.

Garrett set her backpack down and carefully removed the contents. These items were exceedingly rare, not because they were valuable, but because no one wanted or needed them anymore. Refuge was one of the few places they could be found. She unfolded a pair of jeans, real, tangible, cloth jeans, then a black T-shirt. She would need these later.

She turned her attention to the holographic display. It was set up with a Darknet account with a built-in anonymizer that made a lot of privacy promises it could not possibly keep. Still, it would serve its purpose. She addressed the interface.

"Historically, what was Sector 64-N-26-4 in the early 21st century?"

"Sector 64-N-26-4 was known as Portland, Oregon."

The memories came. A vacation. A tour. Something long ago and almost forgotten, but the name was fresh in her memory. Something that others would only stumble over by blind chance, but something she knew from experience.

"Do you have information on the Shanghai tunnels?"

"Affirmative. A group of passages running underneath Old Town to the central downtown section, built to move goods from the docks on the

Willamette to basement storage areas."

Again, the memories took hold. This area had escaped most of the damage from the World Wars but had nearly been destroyed by a tsunami. It was in the rebuilding stage when the sun had released the first Z class solar flare ever recorded, and the associated coronal mass ejection nearly destroyed the planet. Nothing had escaped that disaster and the subsequent destruction unfolded over hours, then days, then weeks, then months as system after system failed. That event had wiped the world clean, removed entrenched interests so others could take over, and the grid had been built on the ashes of that world.

"Historically," Garrett said, "where are we now in 21st century Portland?"

"You are in Old Town."

"Has a GPR survey ever been conducted of this area?"

"Negative. Insufficient cause to use Ground Penetrating Radar."

"Thank you."

The computer went silent, and Garrett settled in for a nap.

There was a small café around the corner filled with people toying with electronic devices, most which appeared to be hand-made. They were inordinately proud of the useless gadgets, gadgets that might serve some minor purpose that the grid could perform a thousand times better. Garrett took a seat at the counter, ordered a synthetic beer, and buried her head in the small holographic display designated for her seat. Her eye movements indicated she was not interested in the various news offerings and the physical manifestation of her disinterest was so pronounced that the slightest pupil dilation settled her on a Japanese anime marathon. She drank the beer as little 3D school girls battled a tentacle monster on the counter in front of her.

A young man sat down next to her and Garrett feigned irritation, glancing at the many other empty seats at the counter that weren't right on top of her. He smiled apologetically, but did not move, activating his own holographic display.

"So you're new here?"

Garrett took a drink of her beer. "Just visiting."

"Interesting place to visit."

Garrett raised an eyebrow. "What are you, grid monitor for the sector?"

"No, no," the man said hurriedly, "nothing like that." The man stared at the holograph in front of him, then turned his head sideways to look at her. "But you are looking for them, aren't you?"

"I don't know what you're talking about," Garrett said, staring solidly forward.

"Right, right," the man said uneasily, and the two fell into silence.

Garrett took another drink of her beer and turned her shoulder to the man since she could not turn her back. He seemed willing to try and breach her nonverbal barrier.

"Look, I might be able to help you…"

Garrett whirled on him. "Just shut up. I don't know what you're talking about," she whispered furiously.

"Fine, fine," the man said, getting to his feet and holding his hands out as if in surrender. "My mistake."

"Everything alright?" the bartender asked, watching the young man hurry from the café.

Garrett downed her beer and wiped her mouth. "Yeah. It's fine. Another, please."

The beer was delivered, and Garrett waved her palm over the light beam on the bar.

"Getting kind of low on credits," the bartender said. It was his responsibility to keep an eye on things, to cut people off gracefully before the system cut them off cold.

"Yeah, I know," Garrett said, "I've got a deposit coming in few days."

"Okay," the bartender said in a tone that indicated he heard that all of the time.

Garrett downed half the beer. "So what was that?" she said, waving her hand toward the recently vacated chair next to her. "Was that guy some kind of narc or what?"

"I don't know," the bartender said. "You some kind of hacker?"

"Maybe," Garrett replied.

That was interesting. It was the bartender's experience that the bad ones always said yes and the good ones always said no. The really good ones always hedged their bets.

"Be careful then," he warned. "A lot of good hackers around here just wind up dead."

Garrett attached the Quinone organic battery to the controller. The controller was scavenged from a cleaning robot that utilized radar to navigate. Next was the low frequency antenna she had removed from a discarded communication bot. Last was the "data processing unit," which was really an outdated gaming device, one that used 2D projection to simulate 3D as opposed to genuine holography. The antenna would receive the electrical pulse from the controller, amplify it, send it downward in a cone, and the gaming device would measure the time required for the return of the reflected signal.

In short, Garrett had just created her own Ground Penetrating Radar. She examined the device, tested it on the floor beneath her, then was satisfied with her work. She stuffed the device into her knapsack, then went to take a very long walk.

The walk was successful, although Garrett had the distinct feeling she was being followed. She did not tarry any longer than necessary, gathered her data, and made it back to the hotel. The homemade GPR confirmed the historical accuracy of the earlier obtained report: the Shanghai tunnels were directly beneath the area. Even more fortunately, there was an ancient entrance to the tunnels in the bowels of the hotel, probably unknown to all inhabitants. From what Garrett had seen, the basement received little if any foot traffic. There were no public cameras within the hotel; she had only to reach the basement unseen and her movement from room to basement would go unrecorded.

She waited until the hotel grew very quiet, then removed her AR jumpsuit and pulled on the jeans and T-shirt. She then removed a strange looking device from her backpack. It was a mask with two, smaller half spheres that looked like eyes and some crudely embedded circuitry. She lay down in the bed, placed the mask on her face and slowed her breathing until it was deep, steady, and rhythmic. She then gave a mental command, waited a second, then removed the mask and laid it next to her on the pillow. The mask emitted a reassuring green light, so she got to her feet, slung her backpack across her shoulder, and was out the door.

Two of the members of Echelon watched the readouts with disbelief, one with a cold expression.

"She was right," Sanction said at last, "her exploit worked."

Arbiter wiped the sheen of greasy sweat that had gathered on his upper lip.

The Intermediary stared at the display, the uninterrupted vital signs, then turned to the senior member of SCAR who was standing by. He was utterly pale.

"You will see that that the engineers develop a patch for this security flaw immediately."

"Of course, your excellency.

The man scurried from the room, grateful that he was not going to be retrained. Although retraining was never supposed to be used as a punishment, he had heard stories where that edict had come down from Echelon.

Sanction stroked his thin lips. "So Zen 12 is off the grid, albeit only briefly. Do you trust her?"

"I don't have to trust her," the Intermediary replied. "Need I remind you that Zen 12 is never truly off the grid?"

Garrett reached the basement without difficulty. The hallways were nearly empty and she avoided the one person still out-and-about by ducking into a shadow. In the cellar, she found the metal plate that sealed the entrance to the tunnel; no one had entered by this route in centuries. She took out a pocket laser and the thin blue light easily sliced through the steel cover. She pulled the cut piece of steel from the hole, set it gently on the floor, then bent down and slipped through the narrow door. She dialed the intensity down on the laser, spread its beam, and used it as a flashlight. She started down the musty passageway.

"We have someone in the tunnel."

"What?" the watch leader exclaimed, and moved to the holo-display. "What the fuck?"

It was a woman, calmly and casually making her way down one of the distant passageways. She was focused, looking for something, and it was unlikely she was out for a stroll.

"Full body scan, see if it's a Guardian or a Keeper."

The subordinate made some gestures in the air, then stared at the data, baffled.

"She's not a Guardian or a Keeper. In fact, she's not wearing AR equipment of any kind."

"What?" the watch leader repeated.

"She has the corneal implants, but—"

The watch commander was analyzing the scan with as much disbelief as her subordinate. "But they're not transmitting," she murmured, "they're fully offline."

The sudden lights blinded Garrett and she dropped her laser and held up her hands.

"I'm not armed," she said.

"Yeah," one man said, "we know. But keep your hands where we can see them."

Garrett lowered her arms but complied with the order. As her eyes adjusted to the bright light, she saw that the three accosting her were definitely armed, all carrying pulse rifles pointed directly at her. The nearest grabbed her arm roughly. "Come along."

The two men fell in beside her, one taking each arm, and the woman prodded her back with the barrel of the rifle.

"I won't resist," Garrett said, and something in her calm tone caused the three to lessen their abuse. They did not lower their guard, but their fear of the interloper diminished.

She was led into a small room with only a table and three chairs. It was dimly lit and the walls and ceiling were padded with a gray porous material with which Garrett was familiar: they were acoustical tiles, designed to dampen and absorb noise. The lead man pointed to the lone chair on the far side of the table and Garrett sat down. The three stood, staring at her.

"And who the fuck are you?"

"My name is Garrett. And you are?"

The man was engaged in some sort of internal struggle because the query was so benign he felt himself responding.

"My name is Porter," he said gruffly. "This is Jani, and that's McKinley."

Garrett nodded politely as Jani and McKinley looked at Porter as if he had lost his mind.

"What are you doing down here?" Porter demanded, trying to regain the upper hand.

"I'm looking for something," she said, carefully assessing the three, "something I'm not really willing to talk about unless I've found it."

McKinley was digging through Garrett's knapsack and came out with a gadget that looked like electronic garbage. "What is this thing?"

"It's an antenna stuck to a battery stuck to a HobbyCube," Garrett replied.

McKinley was dismissive of the device and started to toss it to the side, but Jani took it from him.

"Wait a minute," she said, examining the various parts with interest. "Did you make this?"

"I did," Garrett said, "it's how I found the tunnels."

"What is that thing?" Porter asked Jani.

"It's a homemade GPR," Jani said with admiration, "made out of complete junk."

The three turned back to Garrett, examining her closely.

"So," Garrett said, "have I found what I'm looking for?"

Porter grew deadly serious. "How did you get off the grid?"

Garrett was silent for a long moment, in deep contemplation, then took a deep breath. "I copied my sleep biomarkers for three weeks, combined and randomized them into a passable feed, then substituted them in place of the live feed. Sleep follows a predictable pattern, it's the easiest biomarker to fake. The grid thinks I'm asleep in a hotel room."

"That's not possible," Porter said, shaking his head.

"Which part?" Garrett asked.

"Creating the fake feed is do-able, but how did you swap the feeds?"

"A simple subroutine that replaced one feed with the other from one millisecond to the next."

The barrel of McKinley's gun came up as did Jani's. They hovered in Garrett's direction as Porter controlled his sudden surge of fear.

"And where the fuck would you get that kind of code?" he demanded. "If you were capable of writing it, that would mean you were high-level engineer, possibly even senior level."

"No," Garrett said, "I was never anything more than low-level DSA, a peon. And I was discharged, threatened with retraining because I was a bit too 'creative' for them. I write code for Crapville."

This got McKinley's attention and he began laughing. "You work for Candyland?"

"Yeah," Garrett said, having just admitted she helped maintain a theme in which Board Games and Amusement Park rides predominated.

"Oh Jesus," McKinley said, laughing. "And I thought my previous job was bad."

"That doesn't explain where you got the code," Porter said.

"I had an eye injury when I was 14 years old," Garrett explained, "nearly blinded me and destroyed the existing corneal implant. When they replaced it, I was able to record the subroutine that took one offline and activated the new one. I saved the code for years, wondering what to do with it, always afraid that someone would discover that I had it. I heard rumors of this place decades ago, and started trying to find it. I planned everything out, even tested the subroutine ahead of time. I had to clone the identifying data from my own implants to the ones I jury-rigged, and shorten the transition time down to something the system wouldn't notice, but it worked."

"So the grid thinks you're asleep in your bed?" Porter asked.

"Yes."

The three stared at her for a small eternity, and finally Porter exhaled loudly.

"That is fucking brilliant."

Jani and McKinley both murmured their agreement, and Garrett cocked her head to the side uncertainly.

"Well, how did you guys get here?"

Porter appeared almost embarrassed, and McKinley couldn't meet her eye. It was Jani who voiced her disgust.

"We're all fucking dead."

"What?" Garrett exclaimed, then comprehension slowly dawned. "You faked your deaths."

"Yeah," Porter said, "it seemed the only way to get off the grid. I never thought of the sleep thing."

"Well yours is a more permanent solution," Garrett said, trying to sound encouraging, "and mine is pretty dangerous if I get caught."

"Yeah, but you can head back up topside and walk around like nothing's changed," Jani said, making it sound as if they had all regretted their decision at one time or another.

"Speaking of which," Garrett said, "I can't stay here very much longer. My average sleep period is 7.6 hours, and I can't delay much past that."

Both Jani and McKinley looked to Porter for guidance. This was new and uncharted territory for them. Everyone who came down here was dead to the grid. Leaving had not been an option. Garrett made it easy on Porter.

"Can I come back?"

Porter slowly nodded. "Of course. The boss is going to want to meet you."

Garrett returned to her hotel room, unseen, and lay down in her bed. She ran the subroutine and placed herself back online. As previously agreed, she opened her eyes to indicate she was present once more, then allowed them to close. Having been up all night, it was not long before she went to sleep, this time for real.

After sleeping most of the day, Garrett went to the café and ordered some food and a beer at the counter. The bartender was surprised that Garrett's deposit had actually materialized, and served the order without comment. There was no sign of the irritating young man from before, and Garrett returned to her hotel room and meditated until it was again time to go offline. She repeated the procedure, activated the subroutine, and was once more off the grid much to the dismay of engineers a continent away. She stealthily returned to the basement, and soon was making her way through the tunnels to where Jani was waiting.

"Hey," Jani said, "so you made it again."

"Yeah," Garrett said, "the hardest part is getting from my room to the basement without being seen. I don't want to create an anomaly that the system flags."

"I guess your way of doing it is a little dangerous," Jani admitted, still envious. "But we're all dead if we get caught."

"Right."

Garrett followed Jani through the tunnels far deeper than the night before, and they began to come across people. At first there was just one or two, but after a while, there were crowds of them. Some were engaged in different activities, huddled over holographic displays while they digitally poked and prodded the grid, hoping to find some weakness to exploit, hoping to find that holy grail of hacking that would allow them to over-throw the system. There were various power systems cobbled together, rudimentary but functional. Everyone was quite serious.

They passed through an area that must have been designated as living quarters. There were bunks, pallets, hammocks, all sorts of different sleeping arrangements. Makeshift walls were propped up, providing at least the illusion of privacy. People lounged about, engaging in small talk and socializing. All looked curiously at Garrett and Jani as they passed.

They came to an area where more high-tech equipment lined the tunnel walls, and Garrett thought they must be nearing some type of central command. She was escorted into another room lined with the acoustical tiles and Jani was apologetic.

"I have to go. The boss will be here in a moment. Make yourself at home."

Garrett sat down at the table, certain she was being watched and probably scanned with every type of technology available in the underground bunker. She crossed her arms comfortably over her chest and leaned back in her chair. She didn't have to wait long. The door behind her opened and a muscular man with a beard came in, taking the seat across from her. He held out his hand.

"My name is Morpheus."

Garrett shook the hand. "Shouldn't your skin be a little bit darker?"

The man chuckled. "Familiar with the classics, I see. Yes. I should be much darker than this paleness, and you should have taken a red pill to get here. Instead, you used a hack that no one else ever thought of."

"I had the fortune of nearly losing an eye at 14."

"True," the man agreed, "but social engineering, or taking advantage of what's around you, are all techniques that good hackers use. My real name is Kirkpatrick. I've actually been waiting for you to show up."

Garrett frowned. "Waiting for me. How could you know I was coming?"

"Not many people show up to Sector 64-N-26-4 and begin looking for information on the Shanghai tunnels."

Doubt was evident on Garrett's face. "How did you know I was searching for the tunnels?"

"We've had some small success in penetrating the grid within this sector. Granted, our intrusion is very limited and consists primarily of planting listeners, but it's helpful to eavesdrop on what goes on above us."

"Impressive," Garrett said. "And you've done this undetected?"

"So far, yes."

"Still, a basic search for some ancient tunnels hardly seems proof positive I was coming here."

"No. But added with the fact you created a marvelous device, did your own survey via GPR, and attracted the attention of the local Keepers, all began to tilt the scale toward another convert to our cause."

"What Keepers?" Garrett asked.

"The young man at the café. You were right, he was an informant. He's actually useful in that he weeds out those stupid enough to fall for his fishing expedition. We use him as our first recruitment test. If you actually talk to him, we don't want anything to do with you."

"Hmm," Garrett said, "that makes sense."

"But you'll be our first wanderer, that is, if you want to come on board."

"Of course I want to come on board. I wouldn't be here otherwise. But what's a wanderer?"

"Someone who can come and go at will, someone who can hop on and off the grid. It's been one of our primary goals for decades, and you seem to have found a solution."

"I can't really get on and off the grid," Garrett said, "I can only trick it into thinking I'm sleeping, and only for a short time."

"That's true," Kirkpatrick said. "But we'll figure it out. Would you like a tour of our facility?"

"That would be great."

Garrett followed Kirkpatrick through the twists and turns of the underground tunnels. The walls were stabilized and reinforced. Although much of the equipment was high-tech, all of it gave the impression of hand-made: wires snaked through the passageways until they joined up in tangled messes; compartments were left open and the inner circuitry laid bare; many of the control consoles were physical as opposed to virtual displays.

"Rough, I know," Kirkpatrick said apologetically, "but it works."

"That's all that matters," Garrett said.

There was a canteen area where people were eating.

"Where do you get your supplies?" Garrett asked curiously.

"We're pretty much self-sufficient. About a quarter of our population is devoted to running a biosphere nursery. In fact, we try to think of ourselves as living in a biodome, relying on almost nothing from the surface world. We've excavated far deeper than the original tunnels. They just provided an easy escape for the early settlers of our little colony. Then the hard work began."

Past the canteen were some rooms devoted to machinery, then past that was an infirmary.

"We do have the occasional injury or illness down here, but the infirmary serves more as a cryo-bank than anything else."

"Who is stored there?"

"Just a handful of hanger-ons. Most of us wish to go peacefully into the great beyond, but some will fight it to the end. Zeke there is into his second century, and Ramses is even older than that."

"Do they ever come out of the sleep?"

"Hardly ever anymore. The next time Zeke wakes up, he's probably not going to make it."

"I see," Garrett said. She stared at the cryo-tubes. Each had a placard, and she silently read the names: Zeke, Ramses, Glenn, Alisa, Nika, and Ahab. She was older than all of the inhabitants of those tubes, and felt a sense of compassion. Her longevity had been by accident, not by choice, but these men and women had chosen to extend their lives by skipping large parts of it. True, their rate of decay, to put it purely in mathematical terms, had decreased, but they still slowly aged in the tubes as the world passed them by. As was typical, most of the occupants of the tube were elderly. Cryo-sleep was rarely an option chosen by the young.

"We have numerous research labs," Kirkpatrick said, continuing his tour. "This one here is devoted to bypassing the current reproductive controls."

Garrett nodded her understanding of the implicit goal. Although the original intents of the mandatory, permanent birth control had been noble: population control, increased personal responsibility, the elimination of unwanted births, one of the more insidious results had been unplanned. Because children had to be approved by the Council for Wellness and Development, it ensured they would be tied to the grid upon birth. If these people could somehow reactivate their reproductive potential, they could give birth to a generation that would not receive the corneal implants.

The universal clock hovered above workstations in the lab, and the time caught Garrett's attention.

"I should probably head back to my hotel room. And unfortunately I have to go back to work. Candyland needs some new exhibits. Probably better that I don't push my luck, anyway."

"When will you be able to return?"

"Soon, I hope. I have a lot of vacation built up."

Kirkpatrick, Porter, and Jani watched Garrett disappear down the dark tunnel, and soon, only her laser flashlight could be seen off in the distance.

"If she gets caught, we're all dead," Porter said uneasily.

"No one can withstand a Level 5 interrogation," Jani said, "and that's what she'll get if they catch her."

"Then let's hope she doesn't get caught," Kirkpatrick said, his own unease pronounced. "Let's monitor the chatter from above ground."

Garrett stood before Echelon in full uniform, patient beneath their perusal.

"So you don't believe that any of these so-called hackers are suspects, or useful in any way," Sanction said.

"Correct," Garrett said. "I reviewed the files on everyone in Sector 64-N-26-4B prior to going in, and they were all much as described. Deluded, misguided, but essentially harmless."

"Even though they put a pulse rifle to your head?" Arbiter said.

"I was not in any danger."

"The Senior Engineer was most grateful that you identified such a significant flaw in the system," the Intermediary said.

That was likely untrue, Garrett thought. Anger, terror, even shame, probably accompanied the revelation, but gratitude was unlikely.

"The exploit has been patched," the Intermediary continued. "It will be open to you and you alone if you feel the need to return."

"Understood. I don't know if that will be necessary. I told Kirkpatrick that repeated return trips would be dangerous and he agreed. He said he would send me a message via a 'safe' channel if he wished my return."

"So what exactly did this little jaunt accomplish?" Sanction said.

Garrett was composed beneath the mockery. "I successfully infiltrated their organization and have gained their trust. I eliminated a number of suspects. I have left the door open for return at any time. Beyond that, very little."

The Intermediary's eyes flicked to the displays behind Garrett, the scan of the central nervous system that was excellent at detecting deception. Zen 12 was not lying, and the Intermediary had never known her to lie. Rather it was a subtle withholding of information. Her gaze settled on Zen 12 once more, and one fine eyebrow arched upward. For those who knew the Intermediary, it was as deadly a sign as the drumming of the fingertips.

"But?"

Zen 12 frowned slightly and Arbiter leaned forward, for it was unlike the Guardian to display any emotion.

"But I feel like I've missed something," Garrett said. "Something that was right in front of me."

"The record of your mission has already been analyzed," Sanction said, "and the analysis agrees with your assessment. Little was accomplished."

The Intermediary stared at Zen 12 awhile longer, then waved her hand. "You are dismissed."

Garrett bowed low and excused herself. Once she was gone, Sanction let out a rude noise.

"I dislike 'gut feelings' and other pseudo-scientific nonsense."

"We learned long ago not to dismiss the second mind," Arbiter reminded him. "The neurotransmitters in the gut dwarf those in the brain."

"Yes," Sanction admitted, "that's true. But intuition is just a little too touchy-feely for me."

"And yet no one possesses it to the degree that Zen 12 does." She stood, her robes flowing around her as she turned.

"Have the surveillance of Sector 64-N-26-4 increased," she said over her shoulder, "both sections A and B."

CHAPTER 7

THE RUSTY DUCK WAS ALMOST empty. There were a few patrons downstairs lethargically copulating with one another, but it was a typical sparse crowd for so early in the morning. Dan stood watch at the door, looking bored, and both Duke and Rachel were behind the bar washing up.

Garrett sat in the corner drinking a synthetic Coca-Cola. Real soft drinks were even harder to find than real liquor, and the synth version tasted only slightly different than the real. Most of the world's cinnamon, one of the "secret" ingredients of Coke, had come from Sri Lanka and Indonesian countries that no longer existed. Some still grew in parts of China, but not well, and therefore was prohibitively expensive. Cinnamon could be manufactured from its constituent molecular parts by food dispensers, but to Garrett, it never quite tasted the same.

She ran her fingers over the smooth surface of the wooden table, enjoying the multitude of imperfections that not even time could wear away completely. Although it looked as if she were deep in thought, she wasn't really thinking much of anything, and this nothingness had taken decades to acquire. Rachel occasionally glanced over, smiling to herself at the rather dreamy expression on Garrett's face. It was hard to describe, not one of absence, but rather one of absolute presence. No one was "here" the way that Garrett was "here."

Garrett's gentle caress of the wood slowed, then stopped. Her forearms lay on the table in front of her. She was both slender and muscular, so her veins stood out on her arms. And on her right arm, a pulse of light traveled up the vein of her hand, then to her forearm, then disappeared into the sleeve of her upper arm. It was followed by a similar pulse of light that navigated the veins of her left arm. Without hesitation, she stood up.

"Rachel, I have to go. I'll settle my tab later."

"Sure, sweetheart, no—"

But Garrett was gone, and Rachel had never seen anyone move so fast without appearing to hurry.

Garrett sprinted through the streets of Refuge, not because she needed to, for the transport that was surely coming would find her wherever she was. She ran because she did not want the residents of Refuge to have their peace shattered by the hovercraft that would cause real damage to the aging structures, would kick up real dust that could blind people. As a Guardian, she would protect the non-illusion of Refuge as vigilantly as she would the many illusions of the grid.

She ran through the scanners at the edge of town and then into the gatehouse. The Keeper on duty watched as the object of his incessant curiosity was finally doing something to warrant it, and he peered around the corner as she ran into the locker room. His current theme was World War V, so when she ran back out, she wore the uniform of a General of the North American Alliance. He nudged his fellow Keeper, who was on the same theme.

"See, I told you." He was a mere Alliance corporal while his partner was but a private. "I told you she was someone important."

"That doesn't necessarily mean anything," the private disagreed. "Everyone gets their turn to be a big shot in the rotation."

An enormous craft came out of the sky with a roar, then hovered just above the gatehouse. A stairway unfolded and the Alliance General took the stairs two at a time until she disappeared inside. The stairway retracted, the door closed, and the ship spun about and shot northward at incredible speed. It was gone as quickly as it had arrived.

The Alliance soldiers stood with their mouths gaping, and for once the private agreed completely with his corporal.

"Report," Garrett said calmly.

Mike and Char were both flustered. Although both were seasoned Guardians, a Class 5 alert was a rare and catastrophic event.

"We were at HQ and the entire place was put on high alert about 12 minutes ago. We received no information other than an order for your immediate retrieval."

"From?"

"Echelon."

"I haven't received any orders or information," Garrett said.

"Then how—?" Char started, then stopped herself. She wanted to know how Garrett knew she would be needed, but Echelon had its claws in Zen 12 unlike any other Guardian. Besides, she knew the boss would say nothing.

"It's a system-wide alert," Garrett said, now monitoring her own internal communication channel, "but there's no information available as to cause."

"I guess you get to find out in person," Mike said without a trace of envy.

Garrett strode into the Assembly Room exactly 19 minutes and 36 seconds from when the pulses of light had traveled through her veins. The Council was seated and waiting.

"Perhaps we should require you to reside on-site so that you are more readily available."

Again, Arbiter noted the undertone in the Intermediary's voice, the fascinating undercurrent between the all-powerful head of Echelon and Zen 12. Sanction, too, noted the nuance, the words that could be construed as both invitation and threat. He stole a glance at the Intermediary.

"Was my response time unacceptable?" Garrett asked

Arbiter held his breath as the Intermediary parsed the words, seeking any disobedience or sarcasm. There was none, however; it was merely a polite inquiry.

"No," the Intermediary said at last. "It was within parameters."

Garrett bowed.

"There has been another incident, this one of far greater severity."

The Intermediary waved her hand and a holographic display sprang to life beside Garrett.

"This is Sector 66-R-18-9."

Garrett mentally accessed the information on the sector as the scene unfolded on the screen. It was not an isolation sector, but the majority of people lived in a pastoral, rural setting. It was an area that drew those wanting a quieter life, and almost all of the themes reflected that desire. There were people living in small frontier towns, there were people living in the 1950s, there were people living as simple farmers. It would have been impossible to show all of the competing realities in the display in front of Garrett, so Hybrid did the next best thing and presented each person as they saw themselves. It was simple to pick out each theme as a young man in a black leather jacket, white T-shirt, blue jeans, and pompadour walked down the sidewalk with a young woman in a pink sweater and white poodle skirt on his arm. They did not give the cowboy with the spurs and ten-gallon hat a second glance as he walked past them, and he did not look twice at the samurais clothed in kimonos. The view from a public camera, unless specified, was the dominant theme in the area, i.e. what the majority of people were seeing at any given time. This could be comical or even jarring for those viewing the surveillance, given the juxtaposition of what the people were wearing and their surroundings. And as people filtered in and out of the subsector, the world could shift dramatically. At the moment, it appeared the majority were living in a small, Midwestern town sometime in the middle of the 20th century. To Garrett it looked like the people were trick-or-treating, although she had to remind herself that Halloween no longer existed because life itself had become one great costume party.

The scene looked ordinary, everyone moving about one another, yet completely apart. The farmers interacted with the samurais and the cowboy interacted with the 50's greasers, all cocooned within their little worlds.

And then everything changed.

All of the costumes disappeared, replaced by very plain naked people who sought to hide their nudity, even though that nudity was likely an illusion. But it was a forced illusion, that much was obvious as heads began to jerk in every direction in attempt to access the grid. But their attempts were in vain and panic set in. The previous separatism was united by a common fear and confusion. The woman who had been wearing the poodle skirt now pressed her forearm across her breasts as her companion sought to cover his genitals. The cowboy flushed red, wishing for the ten-gallon hat as he covered both front and back. The samurais fled hand-in-hand.

And then it got worse.

"Zombies?" Garrett murmured, prompting glances from both Sanction and Arbiter. They were not familiar with the term.

At the end of the tree-lined street, figures began staggering towards the already frightened people, and their fright went to terror. Putrid flesh fell off in a trail behind the zombies as they reached out with their shriveled arms and made their way toward the cowering naked people. The former cowboy's panic reached its limit and he snapped a signpost off at its base. He began swinging wildly at the approaching horde, and this elicited cries of pain and rage. A farmer used his hoe to take out a trio of the staggering abominations. Soon the street was filled with the naked versus the undead, and the battle was pitched. Very real blood was spilled and many people and monsters crumpled to the ground. After several minutes of the melee, it abruptly stopped as everyone in view collapsed.

"Control of the grid reestablished at 0746 hours," Hybrid intoned.

Garrett examined the prone figures in the re-creation. The simple statement confirmed the impossible: that control of the grid had been lost.

"Replay timeline with AR deactivated," Garrett said, and Arbiter marveled at the calmness in her voice. The Chief Engineer's voice had risen two octaves upon first viewing the incident.

The scene played out again, but this time it was very different. The small town Main Street was very plain. A few of the trees were real, but the facades of the buildings were nondescript; all of the previous detail had been overlaid by AR. The cowboys, samurais, farmers, and greasers were just average people in steel gray and blue jumpsuits. Nothing changed, but everyone began to clutch themselves almost comically given the fact that they were all still fully clothed. Then another group of people, all dressed in the gray and blue jumpsuits, came down the street. They had looks of terror and despair on their faces, although there was no discernible cause for their distress. They held out their arms in supplication, and were met with the steel pole that the cowboy had snapped off. The people, all indistinguishable from one another in their gray clothing, formed two distinct groups and began beating the hell out of one another. Blood flew in every direction as people fled, tried to hide, or just savagely attacked one another. Finally, everyone collapsed as if the master puppeteer had just cut all of the strings of his marionettes.

Garrett was thoughtful. "Hybrid, was this re-creation based on public cameras or individual feeds?"

"Both. The public camera feed was available in real-time, however, the individual feeds were inaccessible during the actual event."

"So the individual feeds were still recording, they just weren't viewable until after the fact."

"Correct," Hybrid responded.

"What was the extent of the breach?"

"A single subsector. All adjacent subsectors were unaffected."

"How soon was the breach detected?"

"Immediately," Hybrid replied, "multiple anomalies were detected although not identified."

"Why not identified?"

"Biometric feedback was temporarily disabled in conjunction with the loss of the individual feeds."

"And the source of the AR that was forced upon them?"

"Currently unknown."

"How many casualties?"

"Eight fatalities, forty-six injuries, eighteen which were critical."

Garrett turned to the Council. "How many people know of this?"

"Too many," Sanction said bitingly. "There will be massive retraining required of all involved save SCAR and a few senior members of DSA."

"The victims?"

"We did not think an on-scene investigation necessary," Sanction replied. "The true investigation will be conducted by the Engineers to determine how the grid was accessed and compromised. The victims have already begun retraining."

Garrett was silent. The actual incident was well-documented. Interviews would not provide much enlightenment. What happened was not really in question, it was the "how" and the "why" that were mysterious. It was that final question that Echelon expected her to address.

"Well?" the Intermediary said at last, impatient with Garrett's internal musing.

Garrett spoke quietly. "Although there is no evident connection between this event and the murder, given the technological expertise required of both, it's likely they are related."

The Intermediary nodded. "Go on."

"Given the escalation in the level of violence and the increasing sophistication of the attack, it's probable that these are the first events of many."

A muscle in Arbiter's jaw jumped convulsively while the hollows in Sanction's cheeks deepened.

"What is the purpose of multiple incidents? Why not one big incident" Sanction asked.

"That may come. But this is a test, or tests," Garrett responded. "The suspect is analyzing the system, finding and exploiting weaknesses. He, she, or they may not be capable of a big event. Yet."

Sanction glowered. The Engineers had posited the exact same thing.

The Intermediary watched Zen 12's biomarkers, and she saw the subtle indicators of the withholding of information.

"Was there another message to you?"

"Possibly," Garrett said. She tilted her head to address the invisible quantum computing presence.

"Hybrid, during the incident, did any of the victims attempt to deactivate AR?"

"No."

The single word hung in the air.

"Would it have been possible for them to do so?"

"Unknown."

"But they didn't even try."

The AI that was Hybrid was not certain if the question was rhetorical, or if it was even a question at all. It seemed more a comment that the Guardian was making to herself, so the computer remained silent.

Arbiter thought the statement was obvious and Sanction gave it little weight. But the Intermediary sat staring at Zen 12 for a very long time.

Garrett knew that the Intermediary would recall her and therefore did not go very far when dismissed. It was but a short while later that she was summoned to the Council leader's private outer forum. The Intermediary still wore her formal robes and Garrett stood before her since she had not been told to sit down.

The Intermediary leaned on her elbow and ran her index finger lightly over her bottom lip. It was another very dangerous nonverbal cue from her, and Garrett was patient beneath her perusal.

"And how is it you were able to respond so quickly?"

Garrett slowly extended her arm, palm up. She clenched the fist and watched the muscles cord and the veins pop.

"I knew of the breach as it happened," she said, flexing the hand. "I could feel it."

Outwardly, the Intermediary was expressionless, but Garrett sensed a dramatic shift in her mood. The powerful council member stared down at the slender, muscled arm with disbelief and the slightest trace of victory. She alone had authorized the experiment a decade ago, against the strenuous objection or Sanction and Arbiter. She did not speak for a very long time, mulling this turn of events.

"Has there been any unauthorized access to my personnel files?" Garrett asked.

"Your files are highly classified," the Intermediary said, her attention returning with laser-like precision. "Echelon has full access; a few members of SCAR have limited access. Requests for access by other departments are numerous, but rarely granted, and then on only a need-to-know basis."

Garrett held out the arm. "Who knows of this?"

"Only Echelon and the head of CWA."

"The surgeons who performed it?"

"Were all retrained or eliminated."

The dispassionate revelation of the brutal outcome gave Garrett pause.

The Intermediary watched her curiously. "You were experimented upon without your permission, made to suffer excruciating pain, and barely survived the ordeal. Yet you feel no anger towards me."

Garrett said nothing as the Intermediary continued, displeased with the equanimity. "They tortured you, beyond what any human should be able to endure, yet you greet their fate with compassion."

The Intermediary's sarcasm was tangible and Garrett carefully chose her words. "Anger has a time and place, a purpose. It serves no purpose here. Besides, they may not have known they were causing me pain."

"They knew," the Intermediary said coldly. "*He* knew."

"It doesn't matter."

The Intermediary began drumming her fingers, an escalation from the stroking of the lip.

"Why do you ask about your personnel files?"

"Two events, separated in time, geography, method, and neither event has anything to do with me, but—,"

The drumming stopped and the Intermediary leaned forward. The Guardian displayed an uncertainty, a sense of vulnerability that was rare, almost unheard of for her.

"But what?"

"This all feels very personal."

"Why?"

"I'm not certain."

For once, the Intermediary was patient while Garrett sorted through her thoughts.

"In the first event," Garrett began, "the sword seemed conspicuous. A real artifact that I would identify and relate to. Something intimately connected to my belief system. In the second event, 'zombies' are an artifact from my time, again, something I would recognize personally."

"It is my understanding that 'zombies' were an archetype representing fears of global annihilation."

"Yes, fears of famine, war, pestilence, natural disaster."

"Fears that were well-founded."

"Yes," Garrett agreed, "it all came true except the zombies. But there's more."

Garrett rubbed her chin, lost in thought, and the unconscious gesture intrigued the Intermediary because Zen 12 did nothing unconsciously.

"The nudity seemed to be another message, almost a commentary."

"Because the people felt shame over imaginary nudity, because they were still fully clothed?"

"That's part of it. But there's another layer beneath that. 'Shame' itself is a layer of reality, an illusion, an imposition over what's really there. Nudity is just people without clothing. How one thinks or feels about nudity is another thing entirely."

The confession, the vulnerability, the exposition pleased the Intermediary as few things could. She stood, smoothing her robes.

Arbiter knew that the Intermediary had recalled Zen 12. He did not feel excluded from whatever conversations thus ensued. In fact, if anything, he felt relieved. As vast as his knowledge and responsibilities were, the Intermediary's grasp, really a term he used with all of its meanings, filled him with unease. He would as soon leave her to her business.

As much as he wished to mind his own business, however, he did note that it was several hours before Zen 12 left the Intermediary's forum.

CHAPTER 8

"IT'S NICE THAT THINGS HAVE settled down," Mike said.

"Yeah," Char agreed, "I thought with the murder and the 'naked zombie' incident back-to-back, we would have had something else happen."

"It wasn't actually the zombies that were naked," Garrett said, to correct the record.

Several weeks had passed and the Category 5 incident had been passed off as a drill. Echelon had, at Garrett's request, allowed Zen 64 and 82 to view the re-creation of the incident since they were privy to the first incident. The Engineers had yet to identify the source of either breach, and the weeks had passed uneventfully. Although those who knew of the breaches were still operating at an emergency level, Garrett slept peacefully in Refuge and her days were routine.

"We've been assigned a patrol of Sector 48-D-11-4," she said, acknowledging the incoming transmission.

Char accessed the sector information and leaned back in her chair. "God, I hate that world more than I hate the Amish. Why do you get stuck with all the shit sectors, boss?"

Garrett gave her a mild look while Mike answered the question. "Zen 12, remember, *12*?"

"Oh, right," Char said, "I keep forgetting how badass our illustrious leader is."

"I'm not certain why we're being sent out in person," Garrett said, examining the cryptic assignment on her internal channel. "The orders don't specify."

Mike had a huge grin on his face. "Time to deliver some cotton."

The open carriage was pulled by two beautiful white horses. The coats and manes matched the white paint of the elegant carriage and the gold halters matched the gilded trim. The carriage pulled up the dirt lane of the plantation while dark figures toiled in the adjacent cotton fields.

An older woman in a flowing gown and sun hat fluttered a fan in the carriage. The horses weren't moving fast enough to create any relief from the oppressive heat. A younger woman sat next to her, dressed in the same type of garb. The enormous black man in the front seat skillfully managed the reins of the horses.

The heat wasn't really affecting Garrett. Her armor, and in fact, every AR jumpsuit had built-in personal climate control. Temperature comfort varied significantly from individual to individual, so the Engineers used a few quirks of the largest organ in the human body to simplify the process. Skin tended to adapt to anything that was constant, but also tended to over-respond to anything that changed. Right now, small temperature pulses were telling her skin it was cool while the built-in heat sink was shuttling heat away from her body. Under duress, the suit would cool her body rapidly and boost this heat transfer, increasing physical performance. If she were near death, the suit would drop her body temperature to 21 degrees Celsius, placing her in a hypothermic state that would allow her brain to survive without oxygen for up to 8 hours.

The carriage came to a stop in front of a magnificent white house. A southern gentleman, dressed in a long-tailed coat, vest, shirt, and trousers tucked into shiny, knee-high black boots, came leisurely down the steps. His leisure was a sharp contrast to the speed of the young black boy who sprinted over to take the reins of the horses.

Garrett, still fluttering her fan, stepped down from the carriage with the help of the large black man. He assisted the younger woman as the matriarch glanced around the farm. There was little expression on her features as she examined the entire scene. When augmented reality first began to take hold, the idealists said it would usher in a new age, the next step of evolution in humankind. They waxed poetic on the learning opportunities that would arise, the novel implementations of this revolutionary technology that would change the world. It would open eyes, broaden minds, and bring about a brighter, better future for everyone. And in some ways, and for some people, it did. But like the early internet, confirmation bias took hold. People sought out only the information that confirmed their own beliefs, opinions, and prejudices. And where confirmation bias on the internet built a worldview, on AR it built a world.

Garrett was looking at one of those worlds. Despite all of the death and destruction, despite all of the passage of time, despite the massive upheaval of the entire world, parts of the deep south had been immune to change. The rest of the world experienced little racism. Almost everyone was multi-racial to begin with, and AR made real race fairly meaningless. But there was a group of individuals who perpetually believed in their own superiority, despite all evidence to the contrary, and they handed their prejudices down generation-to-generation.

At first, they had petitioned for a permanent distinction on the AR jumpsuits, much like the one that signified biological sex, identifying the race of an individual, or at least whether or not someone was "white." This request was greeted with hilarity by the Engineers because "white" was almost impossible to define, and even if certain DNA categories were set up to identify "whiteness," most of the people who sought this identification probably would not qualify based on their genetic material. The request had been soundly rejected.

The "Sons and Daughters of the Confederacy," as they called themselves, then petitioned for an isolation sector and a theme. This request was considered far more seriously despite its abhorrent character. The grid valued only efficiency, and in the end, the Engineers and techno-psychologists agreed that this was probably the best way to keep this contagion in check. Total elimination had also been discussed, but human life, outside of its sacrifice in the preservation of the grid, was highly valued.

One great difficulty in setting up the sector was the fact that participation was voluntary and all interaction was consensual. And despite the myriad rationalizations of southern scholars on the docile nature of the Negro, the simple fact remained: no one wanted to be a slave. And this was a problem for people who wanted to live in the deep south prior to the

Civil War.

Garrett glanced out to the fields at the dark-skinned men and women dressed in rags who sang cheerfully as they performed back-breaking labor. They moved with a supple grace, but Garrett knew that was one of the greatest illusions of all. She gave the mental command and deactivated AR on her individual visual plane. The field hand sitting on the horse was now dressed in a gray and blue jumpsuit. Much of the detail of the scene was washed out into shades of gray, and the slaves now moved in a jerkier, more mechanical way.

They were robots, automatons that filled a role that no one wanted and that never really existed in the way these people wanted to believe it did. Not one of them was human.

Robotics had not progressed the way that the experts thought it would in Garrett's youth. The technology was extraordinary, and robots performed innumerable functions within the grid such as construction, maintenance, and repair. But they did so on a nanorobotics scale. On a larger scale, it was unnecessary and even undesirable to make them look human. There was no need for a humanlike robot to pilot a hovercraft when the hovercraft itself was the robot. In those few instances where they needed a robot to look human, it was simpler to just overlay AR upon them.

And that was exactly what was being done in the southern sector. When Garrett re-activated her AR, the robots morphed back into so-called living, breathing slaves.

"As I live and breathe, if it's not Miss Willow and Miss Emily. I haven't seen you in ages."

The man in the white coat-tails had finally reached their carriage. Garrett, responding as Miss Willow, fluttered her fan. "Mr. Deacon, it's a pleasure as always."

"And what brings you to our parts this fine day?"

"We had a bumper crop come in, and thought we might share some of our bounty," Miss Willow said in a gentle drawl, "at a fair price, of course."

"You're not foolin' me, my dear," Mr. Deacon said jovially, "You are the wiliest bargainer I've ever seen. Let's go sit and have some tea, talk some pleasure before business." He glanced at the large black man in admiration. "Are you sure you won't bargain for your Negro? He's a handsome buck, prime breeding stock. I bet he could knock up half the gals in this place."

"I assure you," Miss Willow said, fluttering the fan, "my Negro is not for sale."

The two women were escorted out onto the veranda while the large black man joined the other slaves. Iced tea was brought out and the discussion revolved around pleasantries. Mr. Deacon sipped the mint infused beverage, then wiped his long moustache with a cloth napkin. A young man dressed in an outfit almost identical to Mr. Deacon's appeared, although he wore only the vest and had his shirt sleeves rolled up.

"Miss Emily, this is my son Grady. Perhaps he could show you about the plantation?"

Miss Emily rose and took the arm so gallantly presented to her. "It would be my pleasure," she said, and the two strolled away.

Miss Willow lightly slapped Mr. Deacon's sleeve. "Now Duke, get that hopeful look off your face. Miss Emily is still young, and Grady's not much older. Get that idea out of your head."

"Am I that obvious?" Mr. Deacon said. "It's about time for my son to settle down and good women are hard to find these days."

Garrett kept her expression neutral, unwilling to speculate on the root cause of the scarcity of "good women" in the locality. Zen 64 and 82 were patrolling the property, and she could now interrogate "Mr. Deacon" by engaging in mindless gossip. When he proffered his arm, she took it, and they, too meandered about the plantation. Mr. Deacon prattled and Miss Willow gently inquired into anything and everything that might require the presence of the most experienced Guardian in the world. She could determine nothing. Even when they stopped in front of the beating and lynching of one of the slaves, as horrifying as the scene was, Garrett dispassionately dismissed it as insignificant, at least in terms of her current objective. Mr. Deacon watched the lynching with avid interest while Miss Willow plucked his sleeve.

"I'm going to go talk to Miss Emily over by that tree," Miss Willow said, and Mr. Deacon nodded, chuckling at the gentle constitution of women.

Garrett approached Miss Emily and spoke to Grady. "Might I speak to Miss Emily alone, Grady?"

"Of course, ma'am," Grady said, and went to watch the lynching in a manner so casual most would have considered it obscene.

"Have you discovered anything?" Garrett asked.

"A newfound distaste of this sector," Miss Emily replied. "But nothing that would warrant our presence. And 'our Negro' has come up with zero as well."

Garrett quietly assessed the fields as she fanned herself. It was not unusual for her to be sent on assignment without direction, in fact it was standard procedure. Whatever SCAR wished her to find, change, prevent, manage, or correct generally became evident to her. They had learned over time it was best just to set Zen 12 in motion.

"It's strange," Garrett mused. "Normally something will jump out at me, but this is all status quo for this sector." She turned her attention back to the lynching, which seemed finally to be at an end. Mr. Deacon began lecturing the other slaves in the vicinity, telling them that the contrived punishment was a lesson and a warning. Garrett ignored him, but her eyes did settle on the slaves near Mr. Deacon. They had sullen looks of discontent, even anger, as they shuffled about the plantation owner.

"Now that's unusual," Garrett said. She waited to see if any anomalies were triggered, but all alarms were silent.

The anger in the slaves' eyes simmered, seethed, and slowly began to boil as Mr. Deacon pontificated and the overseer stroked the handle of his whip. Grady stood with his hands on his hips, legs spread wide, glaring at his property with arrogance. All seemed oblivious to the growing discontent of their slaves, unaware that they were being surrounded and were greatly outnumbered.

"—and you will keep in your place, will obey your master—"

Some of the house slaves, dressed in maid's uniforms, were coming down the stairs in a slow, menacing, shamble.

"—remember that I feed you, I clothe you—"

Miss Emily looked to Miss Willow for direction. Garrett usually acted instantly, but she seemed willing to let this one play out.

"Are you able to deactivate AR on your personal feed?" Garrett murmured to her.

"Yes."

"Globally?"

"No," Miss Emily said with growing surprise, "I've lost that capability"

"Can you control the slaves?"

Miss Emily's head ticked to the side. "No," she said, the surprise now full-fledged concern. "I can't."

Garrett looked over at "her Negro," who was monitoring their internal communication. He silently shook his head.

"—and you take advantage of my kindness, my generosity—"

The "dead" slave behind Mr. Deacon, the one with the noose around his neck, began to twitch. His eyes opened and he snapped the restraints on his wrists. He then reached up and began pulling at the rope.

"What the hell?" the overseer said.

Mr. Deacon turned at the exclamation and at last shut up. He stared in shock and disbelief as the slave he had just lynched clawed the rope back over his head. The skin was torn and bloody where the rough rope had bitten into his skin, and as he dropped to the ground, a bit of saliva dripped from the corner of his mouth. His yellowed eyes glared with hatred at his master.

Grady screamed as three slaves grabbed him and the overseer went down in a pile of bodies. Mr. Deacon began running, pursued by five field hands. With a total lack of chivalry, he ran right towards Miss Emily and Miss Willow, leading the revolting, violent pack directly at them. Miss Willow was remarkably cool, examining the approaching horde with mild interest. There was a high probability that the pack would take down Mr. Deacon prior to reaching them, but his cowardice gave him a burst of adrenaline and a burst of speed. He was able to put some distance between himself and his pursuers as he ran right past the two women.

"Enough," Garrett said quietly but firmly, and a blue EMF wave rippled across the plantation. The slaves came to a stop and froze. Those holding Grady released him and he straightened his clothing with fearful indignation. The bodies piled on the overseer all slowly removed themselves and got to their feet. The shambling house servants stopped in place. Grady, infuriated at the insult to his honor, turned to slap the slave nearest him.

"I said enough!" Garrett said, "and I meant you, too."

Grady turned on Miss Willow in fury, but his fury was extinguished by ice-cold fear.

The two women in their flowing gowns had disappeared and been replaced by two Guardians in their distinctive black and gray armor. Miss Emily, astonishingly, was an enormous black man, but it was the second Guardian that was arresting in every way. Grady swallowed hard as a third Guardian joined the first two. Mr. Deacon had finally stopped running and was now making his way back to the clearing, more terrified of the three figures that stood there than he had been of the angry mob.

"I—, I—," Mr. Deacon said.

"Be silent," Garrett ordered. "And go over there."

Char turned her back on the plantation owner. "What the hell just happened, boss?" she asked under her breath.

"It was another breach," Garrett said, "one that we were obviously meant to see."

"I was dead in the water," Mike said. "I had no control of the slaves or global AR."

"Could you deactivate your individual feed?"

"Yes."

Multiple hovercraft appeared on the horizon and Garrett nodded to the three men. "Question them and prepare them for debriefing with DHWB. Secure the area and assist the Engineers with the automaton units. I," she said without surprise, "am being recalled."

"What happened?"

The Intermediary's fury was evident. Garrett stood before Echelon, having been transported directly to the nerve center.

"It was another breach," Garrett said. "There was no loss of life in this event, but it's the most severe yet."

"Really?" Sanction said sarcastically, "we lose control not only of the AR but the functionality of the Guardians themselves, and you categorize this as severe? I categorize it as a catastrophe."

"I was able to regain control of the automatons and I don't believe my control of AR was ever compromised."

"Yes," Sanction said bitingly, "but you can't very well be everywhere, now can you?"

The Intermediary sat back in her seat and tented her fingers. "Which brings to mind the most obvious question, what were you doing in that sector?"

Garrett wrinkled her brow, uncertain of the Intermediary's intent. "I was responding to orders."

"Orders from whom?"

Now Garrett was genuinely confused. All of her orders, even those from other sources, were cleared by Echelon. "The orders came from SCAR."

"We have no record of any orders from SCAR."

"They came to me on my internal feed."

All three members of Echelon glanced to the biomarker displays floating behind Garrett, but the Guardian displayed no signs of deception.

"Did you retain an authentication code?"

Garrett mentally accessed the information. "Yes, it is 6AB4329."

The Intermediary sat back in her seat, her eyes on the Guardian, and the room grew very quiet. Garrett did not move, her gaze was steady, and her breathing was slow and regular. The low hum in the forum was the only sound. When the Intermediary spoke, her words were deliberate and a dismissal.

"Resolve has requested your presence at DHWB. You are due for your standard examination with him."

Those who did not know Zen 12 would notice no reaction at all. But one member of the council saw the muscle jump in her cheek and noted the faintest increase in heartbeat in the displays behind her.

"Very well," Garrett said, bowed, and left the room.

"Resolve must be overjoyed," Sanction said when Garrett was gone.

Arbiter shifted in his seat and stroked his jowls. "The authentication code is legitimate, but unidentified. How can that be?"

"The answer to that is more troubling than the question," the Intermediary said. "That authentication code is over a hundred years old."

CHAPTER 9

THE DEPARTMENT FOR HEALTH AND WELL-BEING, or DHWB as it was commonly known, was a colossal facility located a short distance from the buildings housing Echelon and SCAR. All of the buildings in the area were architecturally similar, and they stayed that way as AR was highly regulated within the world capital. But each building seemed to possess an aura, a projection not due to AR, a personality of sorts. Echelon's building, REACH, exuded power, it was intimidating, it was awe-inspiring. The Department of Statistical Analysis radiated emotionless efficiency, constant vigilance.

But the Department of Health and Well-Being was different: it felt sinister, invasive something that could get under your skin, crawl around, and then settle inertly there. People didn't actually express any of these opinions, of course, because that was the quickest way to get an invitation to DHWB.

Garrett stood before the archway of DHWB and felt none of these things. She, more than anyone, had a reason to fear this facility and the people within. But it was just a building, and all of her closely monitored vital signs confirmed her calm as she walked beneath the arch.

A thin, cadaverous man was waiting for her, an extraordinary honor that few wanted. This was Resolve, the head of The Council for Wellness and Adjustment, or CWA. In appearance he was much like Sanction, sharp features, thinning hair, but Resolve had an oiliness about him, an unctuous quality that was absent in the dryness that was Sanction. Resolve was one of the most powerful figures in the world, right behind the three that sat on the high council. As Chief Techno-Psychiatrist, he was the head of CWA, but also a member of SCAR, positions and honors once held by Sanction.

Several senior psychiatrists working in front of holographic displays glanced up from their duties. Resolve disdained almost everything and everyone, but his fascination with the Guardian was well-known. This fascination had more than once been her misfortune, such as the time he stood by her bed for hours, captivated by her tolerance for pain. He had been the one to suggest she be retrained when she passed the Advanced Turing Test. Only the Intermediary kept Zen 12 from Resolve's clutches, for given free rein he would have imprisoned her, experimented upon the Guardian endlessly, then eventually had her euthanized to study her brain. Resolve's brilliance and expertise caused the governing bodies to overlook his streak of sadism.

A sadism that was tangible at the moment as he looked upon his next subject with near glee. The person standing before him was both a fascination and a frustration, a puzzle and a perplexity. And all who were watching thought that the Guardian bore Resolve's obsessive interest with a stoicism that was astonishing.

"Resolve," Garrett said, bowing slightly.

"Zen 12," Resolve said, his pleasure pronounced. "Once again you have failed to take advantage of the health services at your disposal."

"You seem to monitor that for me," Garrett replied evenly.

"Yesss," Resolve said, drawing out the word. "Come along now."

Garrett walked into a room embedded with circuity. The primary purpose of this room was to analyze every aspect of the person being interviewed. Body temperature, galvanic responses, facial expressions, body language, eye movement, speech patterns, brain activity, all were evaluated in addition to the myriad of biomarkers that were monitored all the time.

"Please sit down."

Garrett did so and sat serenely while she was bathed in blue light, then green light, then finally red light. Resolve examined the readouts with a religious-like fervor.

Neuroscientists used maps that predicted almost everything: intelligence, creativity, abstract reasoning ability, tendencies toward addiction or violence. At one time, these neural maps had been misused. Discrimination was rampant and some had even been proactively imprisoned. Now the neural maps were used by the grid to gently influence individuals into appropriate themes, and occasionally for occupational screening. Engineers were especially vetted, but no one was as scrutinized as closely as the Guardians.

Although he had seen it a thousand times, Resolve was riveted by the strong connection between the frontal and parietal lobes. The anatomical pathways that snaked through the flesh complimented and supported the rhythmic activity in the sensory regions. Although it was technically not within his purview, it was within his authority, so he accessed data on her physical condition. Various gas sensors within the AR suits monitored a multitude of indicators: breath, urine, sweat, bacterial composition of microbiome, and therefore were able to detect everything from a UTI to ketoacidosis. Zen 12, as usual, was in perfect health.

"Excellent," he said, sounding slightly disappointed as he sat down across from her. "Let us begin. Is there anything that you wish to talk about?"

"No."

"Well," Resolve said, folding his hands on his lap, "there are a few things I wish to discuss."

Garrett gazed at him expectantly.

"Your latest mission, the one on the plantation. You didn't care for Mr. Deacon."

"I did not care for his actions."

"That seems odd given your background, your endless shades of gray interpretation of reality, your unwillingness to pass judgment."

"You misinterpret my belief system. I don't routinely judge things as good and bad because good and bad are contextual. What is 'good' in one set of circumstances might be 'bad' in another. It's a great flaw to confuse the relative and absolute, but that does not mean that the absolute does not exist. There is evil in this world."

"Is that why you waited so long to step in to stop the uprising? Poor Mr. Deacon was chased halfway across his fields and his overseer was injured. It seems like you and you alone could have prevented that."

"The injuries the overseer sustained were minor, and none of them were in any danger."

"But why did you wait?"

"I was purposely delaying action. The longer the incident continued, the more information was generated for the Engineers to study. Had I stopped everything immediately, there would have been very little to analyze after the fact."

Resolve hid his frustration well. The Senior Engineers within SCAR had echoed Zen 12's words and even expressed admiration that she had extended the incident just long enough for them to have usable data.

"In fact," Garrett continued, "had Mr. Deacon not run right at me, I would have let the event continue for some time. He was easily outdistancing his pursuers."

Resolve glanced to all of the data swimming around him. According to the read-outs, Zen 12's demeanor was tranquil, but he could swear he sensed sarcasm in her tone.

"Why did you switch roles for Zen 64 and Zen 82? It would have been made more sense for Zen 82 to portray Miss Emily."

"It is within my authority to assign extreme morphs."

"I am aware of that," Resolve said thinly, "but why did you do it?"

Garrett was silent for a long moment, and Resolve thought she was not going to answer. But when she did, it was with perfect honesty.

"I find it humorous that Mr. Deacon was attempting to marry his son to an enormous black man."

Resolve thought that he at last had something, but as he mentally flailed about, he did not. Zen 12's actions were within her authority, within the scope of her duties, and had not negatively impacted the mission. There was no proof that a different choice would have resulted in a different outcome.

"It's interesting to me," Resolve said, "that your neuro-linguistic behavior causes you to look forward when recalling events, as opposed to the left which is what most people do."

Resolve's abrupt change of subject was a technique he liked to use, even though it had consistently proved useless with Garrett.

"I was taught that the mind itself is a sixth sense, no different than sight, sound, smell, taste, or touch. Thoughts and emotions pass through it the same way light passes through my eyes or sound through my ears."

"A romantic description," Resolve said, "yet one wholly unsupported by research."

"You've spent years studying me, and yet I've just told you everything you need to know."

Resolve was growing angry, and unlike the Intermediary's cool venom, Resolve could become bitter and vitriolic.

"Yes, study you. Like when every painkilling method at our disposal failed in your operation. Anesthesia, molecular inhibitors, nerve stimulation, direct brain stimulation, all had no effect on you."

Garrett remained silent. Resolve liked to remind her of the horrifying event when he was frustrated. He leaned forward.

"I ran you through the EDA the other day, do you know what the system did?"

This was very dangerous territory, but not dangerous to her. The "Estimated Death Algorithm" monitored an individual's health status and could compare it day-to-day to extrapolate the approximate number of years until the person would die. It was especially useful in determining the value of cryogenic storage.

"It threw an exception," Garrett said quietly.

Resolve's response was shrill. "It defaulted to 1000, then threw an exception."

The thin man suddenly stiffened as if struck, a sure sign that he was receiving an important internal communication and was not handling it with the aplomb that Garrett did. There were certain subjects that were off-limits, even to the powerful head of the Council of Wellness and Adjustment.

"Our session is at an end," Resolve said, his bitterness pronounced.

"Thank you," Garrett said, standing. "I feel much better."

CHAPTER 10

THE RUSTY DUCK WAS ALMOST empty when Garrett arrived in late afternoon. The bell on the door jangled as she entered, and only one customer sat in one of the booths. Rachel was behind the counter and Daniel sat in a chair he had tipped back against the wall next to the stairs into the basement.

"Hey darling. What'll it be?"

"Hi Rachel," Garrett said. "I think I'll have an Irish whiskey."

"Hard day?" Rachel asked out of habit, before she remembered whom she was talking to.

"No, it just sounds good."

"You got it."

Rachel poured the drink, and Garrett waved her hand over the light on the counter to pay for it. She made her way across the bar to one of the tables by the window. She sipped her drink, letting her eyes drift around the room. The worn poster on the wall next to her depicted a woman in a short skirt drinking a beer. The edges of the paper were curled and torn. The glassware above the bar was full of different color liquids, reflecting and refracting light, and creating caustic patterns that flickered on the walls and ceiling. AR was very good at emulating such effects, but real light reflected almost endlessly whereas AR calculated what was "good enough." Few but Garrett could tell the difference.

Her eyes drifted over to the other customer. He was not a resident of Refuge; she had noted that when she walked in the door. But he looked far more comfortable than most, reading the menu with interest. There was no tic that indicated he was trying to get back on the grid, he was not perspiring, and his posture was relaxed. He set the menu aside and looked at Garrett.

Garrett did not look away, and neither did the man. He examined her with the same dispassionate scrutiny she had just used on him. Their staring match grew prolonged, as each seemed to absorb the physical presence of the other. Then the man smiled, a smile neither pleasant nor unpleasant, but one with a little arrogance in it. He got to his feet and Garrett glanced over to Rachel. In a few steps, the man was out the door as the bells jangled.

Garrett was on the move to the door with an urgency that Rachel and Daniel had never seen before. She pushed out onto the street as the bells jangled, and looked both ways.

There was no one there.

She ran to the edge of the decking to peer around the corner, then ran to the opposite side and did the same. There was no one on the entire street. Garrett glanced around, her eyes keenly searching in every direction, even upward, and there was nothing. She slowly walked back into the restaurant.

"Do you know who that man was?"

Rachel looked up from her inventory. "What man?"

Garrett silenced herself and carefully thought through her words.

"Was there anyone else in here besides me?"

Rachel looked to Dan for confirmation, and he shook his head.

"There was no one else here but us."

"Did you hear the bells on the door right before I got up and went outside?"

Dan shrugged and Rachel tried to remember. "Yes, no, I mean, I don't know. The wind rings the bells all the time."

"All right. Thank you. I have to go."

In a flash, Garrett was gone, and Dan and Rachel looked after her curiously.

"Well, she just got all professional on us," Dan said, "maybe she's one of those Keepers."

It was a regular topic of conversation for them, trying to guess Garrett's occupation.

"No," Rachel said, picking up an already clean glass and wiping it down. "Those guys at the gate are dicks. She's nothing like that."

It was late in the evening and Char was surprised to see Garrett walk back in the doors of Guardian HQ. Mike had already left for the day, as had Garrett, but here she was returning. She was strolling, not quite hurried, but with definite purpose.

"Everything okay, boss?"

"Yeah," Garrett said, coming through the door. "I just need to take care of something."

She sat down in front of a full holographic console, one that would provide more intensive computation than the usual "heads up" display. There was no program for what she wanted to do. Facial composition software, in a forensic sense, was obsolete due to fact that everything was recorded. No eyewitness statements were ever needed. There was a complete record for everyone on the planet. But although there was no forensic program, there was something available that was probably even better.

"Hybrid, access character creation algorithms for AR."

Char watched Garrett with interest. Zen 12 was always focused, but right now she had a preternatural intensity about her.

"Give me a blank canvas and manual control."

An empty holograph flickered in front of her.

"Begin with head shape."

The display began to cycle through the most common head shapes. Garrett swiped right, left, up, and down to accept, reject, or adjust them as she dialed down into what she wanted. She was able to make manual adjustments with her fingers, resizing the temples and chin. She accepted the match with a tap and the algorithm switched to eyes. She moved through the prototypes in a flurry, so fast that Char could barely make out what she was doing. The algorithm moved to the nose, the mouth, the cheekbones, and at various stages, Garrett would return to an earlier body part to narrow the match down further. She looked like she was conducting an orchestra as her hands and arms moved to manipulate the visage, an orchestra she conducted with startling speed.

Finally, Garrett sat back and stared at the man who had been sitting in the Rusty Duck. His disembodied head floated in front of her.

"Who is that?" Char asked.

"Hybrid," Garrett said, "identify this man."

Hybrid did not answer.

Garrett cocked her head to one side. Not "unknown," or "no match," or even a list of possible close matches. There was simply no response. And in the instantaneous world of a quantum computing, that pause meant that somewhere a human being was involved.

Garrett tried to get her foot in the door before it closed. "Is this information classified?"

"It is beyond classified."

"Beyond classified?" Char said. She had never heard of such a thing. And no one had a higher security clearance than Zen 12.

"You are to report to Echelon," Hybrid said, and the visage Garrett had created disappeared.

Slowly, Garrett pushed away from the console and got to her feet.

"You should go home and get some sleep," she said.

"Right," Char responded. There were many times that she had envied Garrett's easy access to the halls of power. Right now wasn't one of them.

"What were you doing?"

The Intermediary was present in person whereas both Sanction and Arbiter were present by holographic projection. That might have been because the two men were pulled from slumber, or it might have been because they were avoiding the Intermediary's fury.

"I was trying to identify a man I saw in Refuge."

"Play back Zen 12's feed," the Intermediary said icily.

Garrett internally gave Hybrid the time frame and then waited patiently while the scene in the Rusty Duck unfolded. Garrett entered an empty bar, purchased a drink, sat and sipped the drink, stared intently at an empty booth, looked over at the bartender, then ran to the door. She exited the restaurant, looked everywhere at an empty street, then re-entered the bar and engaged the female bartender in conversation.

"Do you know who that man was?"

"What man?"

"Was there anyone else in here besides me?"

"There was no one else here but us."

"Did you hear the bells on the door right before I got up and went outside?"

"Yes, no, I mean, I don't know. The wind rings the bells all the time."

"All right. Thank you. I have to go."

The Intermediary's fingers began drumming.

"At the risk of stating the obvious," Sanction said, "there was nothing recorded on your feed."

"I know," Garrett said calmly. "That was the first thing I checked. I wouldn't have needed to reconstruct the face had it been recorded."

Now Sanction was angry. The fact that Zen 12 was also stating the obvious made it worse.

"Hybrid, replay section," Garrett said, and the scene again unfolded. Garrett entered an empty bar, purchased a drink, sat and sipped the drink, stared intently at an empty booth, looked over at the bartender…

Garrett gave an internal command to stop playback, which made the sound of the bells on the door very loud in the forum.

"Well?" Arbiter said uneasily, "that woman said it could have been the wind."

"None of us were looking at the door," Garrett said, "and there are no public cameras in Refuge. We have no visual record, only auditory."

The room fell into silence save the quiet hum of electricity. Garrett looked at the Intermediary steadily as the fingertips drummed on the table.

"Who was that man?" Garrett said at last.

"That is classified."

It was a non-answer that provided a wealth of information. It indicated that the person did in fact exist. The visage belonged to someone, a someone that Echelon knew. And the Intermediary wanted her to know that they knew, or the Councilor would have denied all knowledge. Or perhaps the Intermediary just suspected that Zen 12 would have detected the deception, even from her.

"Classified to the Guardians?" Garrett asked.

"Yes," the Intermediary said, "even to you. We must discuss this internally," she said, gesturing to her council members. "You will speak of this to no one and the reconstruction you created has already been destroyed. Do you understand?"

"I do," Garrett said, bowing slightly.

"Then you are dismissed."

Zen 12 turned on her heel and left the Council forum.

"This makes no sense at all," Sanction said, "Are you certain your beloved weapon is not losing it?"

He regretted the term "beloved" the instant it came out of his mouth, and he was glad he was not there in person as the Intermediary turned upon him with a look that likely would have melted the skin from his bones.

"I am certain of little at this point," she said scathingly, "but that is the most unlikely explanation of all."

Arbiter's unease had not lessened. "Why not tell her who the man is?"

The Intermediary leaned back in her chair as the visage of the man appeared before them all.

"I want to see how this plays out."

CHAPTER 10

THE HYPERSONIC FLIGHT MADE SHORT work of the distance they needed to travel. At Mach 13, just shy of 16,000 KPH, the plane traveled through the thin air of the upper atmosphere, the AI pilot constantly calculated the positions of the solar balloons, negotiating a path through the floating monstrosities that sent precious energy back down to earth. Although the temperature of the hull was somewhere in the realm of 1900 degrees Celsius, the three occupants of the vessel were comfortable inside.

"A mere Category 2 incident," Mike said. "This should be a piece of cake."

Zen 62 spoke the phrase facetiously. He had picked up the idiom on their last mission, as the expression had its roots in slavery. The sarcasm extended to the Category 2 designation as well. Prior to recent events, a Category 2 incident was considered rare and momentous. Now it seemed common and mundane.

Garrett reviewed the light displays in front of her. The plane was capable of traveling at up to Mach 25, but that was unnecessary, even to travel to the Red Zone, which was halfway around the world. Hypersonic flight had made the world very small, and it was a short trip even to what had once been mainland China.

The Red Zone was full of isolation sectors, and Garrett wondered if that was due to the collective nature of the people prior to AR, as if that tendency was so ingrained it had continued on. In the Blue Zone, isolation sectors were the exception rather than the rule.

Sector 87-X-33-1 was at the very western edge of what had once been China, perhaps even spilling over into the Middle East. Although both Zen 64 or 82 would review the historical record for relevant factors, Zen 12 pulled a few of them from memory. There was a reason why this particular theme had taken hold of here.

The plane descended, its sleek profile cutting near silently through the clouds. They glided in and touched down unnoticed.

"Switching to dominant theme," Char said. She was now wearing a sheath dress, sandals, gold jewelry around her neck, and arm bands of the same simple gold design. Her hair was long and dark and woven with ornaments. Mike was bare-chested, wearing a short, pleated kilt with a gold embroidered belt and sandals. His hair was as long as Char's, and although both had maintained most of their physical characteristics, Char had gone a little darker and Mike and gone a little lighter: both now had brown skin.

Garrett also switched themes. She looked very similar to Char with a slight variation in the jewelry.

"Nice eyeliner, boss," Mike said.

"It looks good on you, too," Char said, retorting for Garrett.

"And I think you're wearing more than both of us," Garrett said, eying him.

They set out from the plane and, had their outfits not given them clue to the current theme, the sight of the great pyramids on the horizon surely would have given it away. The Sphynx had also been reproduced, and in fact all of the great, Ancient Egyptian sites had been recreated, albeit much closer to one another than they had ever been in real life.

Real life, Garrett thought to herself. There was that phrase again, the idea that had already been slippery and now was ungraspable.

"I notice you didn't set up a meet-and-greet with the local authorities," Char said.

"There is no Guardian assigned to this sector. It's monitored entirely by Keepers. Regardless, we'll be going deep cover on this assignment," Garrett responded.

"Something you want to tell us?"

"I have no specific information," Garrett said, "just a hunch."

Mike and Char glanced at one another. "Deep cover" meant they could not be identified if someone chose to deactivate AR. They would not be identifiable even to other Guardians. It was an ability that few had the power to authorize.

Garrett had analyzed all of the data on this sector. Although everything was continuously recorded, that didn't mean it was constantly viewed, at least not by a human being. The AI was very good at sifting through massive amounts of data, identifying trends and anomalies, earmarking statistically significant events. But it was not always capable of understanding the subtleties of human behavior.

At least not yet, Garrett thought. She knew it was only a matter of time. In her extended lifetime, she had seen the original mainframe computers, then saw how the system had decentralized to multiple programs on individual personal computers. With the advent of the internet, it had returned to the mainframe concept with the "cloud." But it returned as something different than simple distributed computing, not just mere electricity spitting out ones and zeroes, but something with cognition. The bigger the cloud, the faster it increased in value, the larger it became. It was a cycle that predicted that in the end, there would only be one grid. And the smarter that grid, the more people used it, and the smarter it grew. What started with "search engines" ended with Hybrid; every single query taught the system. There was no longer a cloud, Garrett mused, it was the entire atmosphere.

The system had flagged this sector as having a number of issues without a discernible cause. Increased dissatisfaction, paranoia, aggression, coupled with an almost contrary passivity and submission to authority. Not the true authority, i.e. the bureaucracies that made up the world government, but the local authority within the theme. When a sector began throwing out such red flags, an investigation was initiated. Although it was possible to go back and review the visual record, this was time-consuming and not always fruitful. It was simpler to send in a Guardian. And when the problem was systemic and serious, they sent in Zen 12.

"Something's definitely wrong here," Mike said.

Garrett glanced around her. They were viewed with suspicion, dislike, something that was unusual even for isolation sectors. It was one of the factors that had leaped out at her: this sector had a 95% persistence rate, meaning less than 5% of the people who lived within the sector ever left it. Of those who left, almost none returned. And because "Ancient Egypt" was an isolation sector, that meant the people here either stayed in Egypt, or went off the grid.

And no one ever went off the grid.

Many of these people had lived in Egypt for decades. Their belief index was very high and they no longer differentiated between the theme and reality. Having seen the phenomenon many times, the techno-psychiatrists had yet to decide if this was a good thing or a bad thing, and the research collected was inconclusive. In some circumstances it led to greater stability and harmony, in others, a rampant xenophobia could take hold.

By the looks of those around her, Garrett thought the latter was occurring. They attracted a great deal of attention; none of it was positive.

"Can I assist you?"

An officious looking man wearing lightweight armor approached them, one of the city guards. Garrett accessed his internal file, noting that he was a senior Keeper.

"No, we are simply visiting."

"And how long will you be staying?"

"A few days."

The guard was undecided. Normally he would harass visitors, try to convince them their presence was unwelcome. But the steady gaze of the woman before him discouraged any such behavior.

"Fine, just mind yourself while you're here."

"And why wouldn't we?"

Such a response should have angered him, but instead he was filled with a strange sense of shame at the mildness of the reply. He made a gruff noise and stormed off.

"Well this is interesting," Char said.

They continued to attract a great deal of attention as they made their way through a bustling marketplace, then on to the temporary housing that had been arranged for them. It was a two-story stone structure, well-furnished and staffed with two servants, a perfect domicile for the mid-level nobility they were portraying. They had no sooner conducted a quick walk-through of the layout when a servant came to Garrett, looking fearful.

"There are men at the front door for you."

Garrett went to the entrance hall, which was now filled with several large men all dressed in the lightweight armor of the city guards.

"Is there a problem here?" Garrett asked.

The head guard, so prepared to intimidate the foreigners, was at a loss. This woman had a serene confidence about her that was disconcerting. She looked at them as if she were a majority of one, and they felt outnumbered.

"No, um—," the guard said, shuffling around. "We were just…"

"Do the city guard welcome all visitors in this manner?"

The question was benign, but it carried the weight of an indictment.

"Of course not," the head guard said, and now all of them were shuffling about, shifting from side-to-side. They were used to uncomfortable situations; they were just not used to being on the receiving end of the discomfort.

"Then, is there something you need?"

"No…" the guard said, drawing the word out for lack of a follow-up.

"Then good day to you," Garrett said, turning on her heel and leaving them to let themselves out. The stunned and confused troop paused for a moment, then left the way they came.

"Hard to believe those were all Keepers," Mike said.

"Yes," Garrett said, taking a seat on the lounge.

"Did they send you for an extraction?" Char asked.

"Not explicitly," Garrett said, "but I have the feeling that's the way it's going to go."

An extraction was the forcible removal of a high-ranking Keeper. A major extraction was the removal of a Guardian, and it was a rare event indeed. To Garrett's knowledge, only four major extractions had been authorized in the last two decades, and she had performed them all. But regular extractions, although still uncommon, were more routine. They weren't going to deal with anyone who could control the grid.

"As usual," Garrett said, "I was given little if any information, simply told to respond to this sector and analyze the situation. I pulled the data profiles of the population and saw the red flags the system was generating. That led me to review the profile of Ammon, which I'm sure you did as well."

"Guy has set himself up as a Pharaoh," Mike said. "Seems to have gone a little native."

"Not only that," Garrett continued, "he's repeatedly requested exemption from rotation, so he's been here a very long time."

"An insular society, an isolation sector, and geographically remote, that's a bad combination," Char said, "but with the scrutiny Keepers receive, it seems like someone would have noticed 'Ammon' was going off the rails."

"I'm sure his handlers are sweating it right now," Mike said.

That was an understatement, Garrett thought. The failure of a high-ranking Keeper was bad enough; the failure to notice it was far worse. It would take multiple oversights for something of this magnitude to occur, and even one was unacceptable to the Intermediary.

"There is supposed to be a grand event at the Sun Temple this afternoon. I suggest we attend. Until then, we should split up and see what we can see."

Garrett wandered about the city accompanied only by one of the servants, more a nod to local decorum than from actual need. She visited all of the obligatory tourist attractions, aware that she was being followed the entire time.

Her eyes missed nothing. Shopkeepers gazed at her sullenly. Vendors eyed her warily. The Guards watched her every move. Servants looked at her fearfully and their masters looked at her with disdain. There was a definite caste system that everyone seemed invested in, even those who did not benefit from it. Garrett marveled that, although the traditional drivers of inequality had been removed, it was remarkably enduring. Most of the people in this sector had been born here, raised in the theme, received all of the state-mandated training, yet none saw any alternatives to their current existence. At one time, there was a debate amongst the techno-psychiatrists as to whether children should be exposed to multiple themes, or required to spend a year in another theme once they were of age, but these initiatives had been abandoned, the reasoning as cynical as the outcome. The decision was phrased in near-incomprehensible jargon, but Garrett had concisely interpreted it. The overall purpose of AR was not to improve humankind, but rather to pacify it, to keep it entertained long enough to avoid self-destruction. Anyone with enough drive to rise above the pacification was drafted into maintaining the system that kept everyone else asleep.

And so despots, cult leaders, and charlatans were paired with their sheep in lovely locales such as Nazi Germany, allowed to do whatever they wanted without physically harming one another, and without physical coercion. But mental and emotional coercion were allowed to the point they did not interfere with life satisfaction or threaten the integrity of the illusion. And humans, it seemed, could be content in the most horrifying circumstances.

Garrett leaned against a pillar engraved with hieroglyphics. And so, someplace in the world, there were Germans happily sending Jewish automatons to their deaths in gas chambers and ovens, allowed to do so because their sickness was contained. And Guardians, Guardians were tasked with maintaining the illusion, balancing the competing illusory worlds while ensuring the safety and satisfaction of the inhabitants of those worlds, regardless of personal feelings of morality. It was an almost impossible job.

And here, Garrett would not be able to simply snap her fingers as a warning, as she had with the Raiders. The Raiders were casual participants, occupants of an isolation sector, but one with a very low belief index and a moderately low persistence rate. It was of no danger to remind them that they were using AR. Their terror was of being off the grid.

These people, however, these people would break. Garrett was very limited in what she could do. Her internal communication with Char and Mike indicated they were experiencing the same cold reception from the local populace, that something important was happening this afternoon, and that they were being pressured to leave before it did. Judging by the overall mood of this city, they had been sent in very late in the game.

Garrett pushed away from the pillar. She would go change into formal wear for the ceremony.

The Sun Temple was magnificent. Its outer walls were square, accurately recreated from all known sources, then embellished as the Engineers saw fit. The raised platform at the far end was superb, and the obelisk at its center was awe-inspiring. Garrett briefly turned off AR, viewing the bland structures, always intrigued by the technology used to create the illusion.

In this case, the stone walls were actual metal, optical meta-metals to be exact, but Garrett was struck by an even deeper layer of illusion. The walls appeared solid, even without AR activated, but in truth the alloys were formed into a grid. The openings, no larger than 700 nanometers and some less than 400, were far too small to be seen. Because this space was smaller than the wavelength of visible light, the light was trapped in the grid and the photons could be stored and manipulated. The technology used to create a world devoid of technology was extensive. Even the "Nile" flooded at regular intervals.

Garrett switched her view back to the dominant theme. A procession was entering the main gate. A huge platform, borne on the backs of sweating men who labored beneath the weight, was carried in. A throne was on the platform, and on the throne was a dark-haired man dressed in the raiment of a Pharaoh. He was surrounded by his concubines and servants.

"He definitely has gone native," Mike murmured into her ear.

Garrett merely sighed. She had seen such ostentatious displays when reviewing Ammon's profile. Although they were not specifically prohibited, they were discouraged unless necessary for maintaining the illusion of a theme. Ammon had provided sufficient rationale, proposing that such displays were integral to the political structure of Ancient Egypt because it revolved around the power of the Pharaoh. And he had further argued that he be the one to fill that vacuum since no one within the city had risen to prominence. He had made these arguments years ago, and for years his reign had gone smoothly.

Until now. This city was on edge, a thin veneer of normalcy overlaying a rising hysteria. It was Ammon's job to calm that hysteria. Instead, he seemed to be its root cause.

The Pharaoh reached the dais and his throne was moved in front of the obelisk. He had remained seated the whole time, and only now rose. He began to address the crowd in a deep, booming voice. Mike and Char moved closer so that they could hear his words, and Garrett followed. She wasn't really listening however; she didn't need to. Over the years she had heard the same words from so many, the same promises and threats, the same pandering to illogical fears, the same demonization of the "other," all parlayed in the same hypnotic voice, full of rhythm and syncopation. And it would have been different had Ammon been playing a role. But Garrett could tell that he was not.

Ammon's gaze swept the crowd as he spoke, and his eyes settled on the three of them. His voice did not hesitate as he attempted to access their identities via internal channels. The Deep Cover algorithm activated, and Ammon saw only three visitors, low-level nobodies on vacation. Still, his eyes lingered on the trio, especially the woman who gazed at him so impassively, unlike the frothing throng around her.

"Did he just say something about human sacrifice?" Char said uneasily. Although Garrett's presence was reassuring, the recent failures of the grid were heavy on her mind. If they lost control of their abilities in the midst of this mob, things could get ugly.

"He did," Mike said, "that is not a good sign."

"Worse," Garrett said, "it's non-canonical. The ancient Egyptians were not associated with human sacrifice."

Mike looked over at his boss. Sometimes it was really hard to tell whether or not she was joking.

Ammon's scrutiny of the trio had grown fixed, and his head priest had noted the attention of his master. He, too, began staring. Those around them in the crowd began to distance themselves, muttering imprecations and making gestures to ward off evil. One even spat in the dust. The priest and a phalanx of guards made their way down from the platform and started to push through the throng towards them.

"Why do I have the feeling this is going to be bad?" Mike said.

"You will do nothing," Garrett said quietly.

The guards and the priest reached them just as Ammon's voice peaking.

"The Gods have demanded that we rid ourselves of this foreign plague, that we purify ourselves with the blood of our enemies!"

The guards snatched Char, who began struggling wildly. Mike went to her aid, but he was accosted by three burly guards who restrained him. Garrett merely watched as Char was dragged kicking and screaming to the platform. She was forced face-down on an altar, her arms held as a burly, axe-wielding guard in a mask stepped forward. The crowd screamed in an ecstasy of blood-lust, and the axe was raised skyward.

Garrett stood amongst the crowd, a solitary, still figure in the midst of a rabid mob. They began chanting as one, demanding the death of the outsider. Their actions were mindless, disgusting, wrong on every level. Garrett was again reminded of Nazi Germany. What would it have been like to stand before them in all their pomp, all their ceremony, all their self-congratulatory parades, to listen to Hitler spew his vitriol and hate, his message of superiority...and snap her fingers and shatter his illusion? What would it be like to exercise that kind of power?

Mike looked over at Garrett.

"Boss, that's a real axe."

"I am aware of that," Garrett said calmly as the axe fell.

Half a world away, the Intermediary sat watching the proceedings on a live feed. The axe fell, the head of Zen 82 was separated from her body, hit the ground with a thud, then rolled off the side.

"I told you she wouldn't stop it," she said, a trace of triumph in her voice.

"Unbelievable," Sanction said. "It seems that once again you know her better than anyone."

The Intermediary was pleased, pleased enough to ignore Sanction's insinuation. She was pleased with the actions of Zen 12 and even more pleased that she had been right.

"Oh dear god," Mike said, and looked to Garrett for some sort of direction. She merely shook her head.

"Bring them!" Ammon commanded. He turned on his heel and headed into the temple. Char's body was unceremoniously pulled from the altar, then dragged along the ground behind his entourage. Both Garrett and Mike were handled roughly, pulled through the hissing, fervent crowd. They, too, were dragged into the temple, although slightly more upright than Char's body.

Ammon settled on his throne, his manner imperious, his expression arrogant, his lips curled into a sneer. He gazed at them, Garrett in particular, with scorn. Char's body was dragged next to Garrett and callously dropped to the ground.

"Leave us!" Ammon commanded, and as his attendants and guards began to leave, his eyes settled solely on Garrett. "I saw you when you first entered the city. Your manner had me concerned. But you are not what I thought you were."

Garrett said nothing, and her silence angered Ammon. Her demeanor vexed him, and the fact that he had no effect on her vexed him even more.

"You have no idea the power that I wield," he said.

"Oh, I think that I do," Garrett replied. She looked over to the dead body next to her. "Char, put your head back on."

To Ammon's astonishment, the corpse rolled over and its head reappeared, then it got to its feet. Garrett snapped her fingers and the blue EMF wave rippled outward, dissolving the surrounding temple into basic shapes and shades of gray. She stood there in her black and gray armor, and was joined by Zen 64 and 82. Ammon's arrogance dissolved into fear.

"How—?" he stammered. "What—?"

"I am Zen 12," Garrett said. "So you were probably correct in your first assessment of me. But you were also right. I am not what you think I am."

Ammon wasn't thinking very clearly. The forcible removal of the AR was jarring, terrifying. His lower lip trembled and he was physically shaking as he looked around the room at the bland grayness, then down at himself. All of his jewelry, his clothing, his muscular physique, all of it was gone, replaced by a thin, aging body in a simple gray and blue jumpsuit. His mind sought to reconnect to anything familiar, and his head began jerking as he fought to get back on the grid that was denied him. This couldn't be real.

Garrett observed the metamorphosis in silence. If even the highest-ranking Keeper within the sector was so within the thrall of AR, deactivating the grid for the population as a whole would have had catastrophic consequences. As difficult as it had been to allow the "sacrifice" to proceed, it had been the correct choice of action.

"Ammon, or should I say Keeper Jones, was it really your intent to kill someone today?" Garrett asked.

Keeper Jones was confused by the question.

"The axe you used was real," Garrett continued, "capable of inflicting actual harm. If you felt a human sacrifice was necessary for maintaining the political structure of Ancient Egypt, that easily could have been simulated."

"Simulated," Keeper Jones said to himself, "simulated."

"Yes," Garrett said, "a simple request made through channels. But I contend that a human sacrifice was pointless. Aggregate biomarker analysis did not support a desirable outcome."

Keeper Jones's jaw worked as if he were physically chewing on this concept. Garrett sighed.

"Keeper Jones, you are charged with violation of Section 2856.5 of the Code of Law and Order. You are relieved of duty."

Keeper Jones, grew pale. Despite the fact that he had been immersed in an ancient culture for years and did not remember the exact code, he recognized the subdivision instantly. All sections within subdivision 2800 of the Code of Law and Order dealt with interference with the grid or failure to maintain the illusion of AR. It would have been a lesser charge to accuse him of the attempted murder of the Guardian he had beheaded.

Garrett was fully aware of this paradox. The Keeper's greatest sin was not that he had tried to kill someone. His greatest sin was that he had lost sight of his purpose, which was to maintain his flock in a passive state of contentment. Had an illusory human sacrifice contributed to that goal, it would have been allowed. A real human sacrifice was unnecessary and worse, inefficient.

"Zen 64, please take this man into custody."

Mike placed Keeper Jones in restraints, altered his prisoner's appearance so that he no longer looked like "Ammon," then escorted him from the room.

"So how do we get this sector back on track?" Char asked.

"I'm going to recommend that Zen 125 be temporarily transferred here," Garrett replied. "She can take Ammon's place and guide the populace back into a more acceptable interpretation of this theme. It will take some time, but I think her subtlety will play well here."

Echelon was pleased with the Guardians' handling of Sector 87-X-33-1. They were even more pleased that there had been no troublesome hiccups with the grid, that the incident had been exactly as presented and nothing more. Sanction dealt with the internal personnel failures that had contributed to the flaws in oversight, Arbiter assigned a handler for Zen 125 as the recommended transfer took place, and the Intermediary rewarded the Guardians with a brief respite from work, although as always, her eyes and sensors were never very far from Zen 12.

CHAPTER 11

THE "CITY" WAS THE EPICENTER of the world.

Simultaneously New York, Paris, London, Hong Kong, or just about any large, urban metropolis from history, it housed the highest population density of anywhere on the planet. A hundred and forty million people lived in a little over four thousand square kilometers.

Garrett stood in the middle of Times Square. The thrum of the city was palpable, both human and mechanical, forever intertwined. Human beings had become batteries, just as predicted by dystopian science fiction, but they weren't housed motionless in pods. Rather all of the energy they generated through normal activity was used. Nothing was wasted. Piezo-electrics were built into everything, harnessing vibration and pressure, converting it to energy. Every surface was solar paneled, every roof maximized its reflective capacity, every drop of water was recycled. The microbes that lived in the public lavatories digested waste and produced electrons. Food waste was fed into digesters that generated methane. Oxygen was generated by calculated optimum photosynthesis, provided by the hydroponics and heliostats on every level of the surrounding skyscrapers. Even water flowing downward through pipes provided energy, captured by turbines that skimmed off excess pressure. The energy generated was colossal, steady, and reliable, and all it had taken to bring this about was the utter and absolute destruction of every self-interested corporation that had powered the world before. Coal, oil, and gas all died fiery deaths, and this world had been built on their graves.

A hot dog vendor hawked his wares on the corner of Broadway and West 46th street. Garrett remembered hot dogs, the real ones, and although most food was now made from crickets or soy products, the present incarnation was a fair representation. And from what she remembered, the past incarnation had more than a few insect parts in it as well. She passed on the hot dog and continued down the street.

She was going to meet Char and Mike at a local club. Her life was such that she did not normally socialize, other than her few forays to the Rusty Duck in Refuge, but it was Char's birthday so tonight she would make an exception. She had about two hours before she was to meet them, and she knew exactly how she wanted to spend them. Her powers as a Guardian were hers to use as she pleased, and she had absolute discretion in that usage. That said, she rarely utilized them outside of a work setting. But today, she was going to make an exception.

She stood on the corner, at the edge of the street, staring out over the vast cityscape that was current New York. She could turn it into Tokyo, or Moscow, or Beijing, but for the moment, New York was fine. It didn't really matter. She gave a series of internal commands to Hybrid, then just stood there, hands in her pockets.

The first thing that was noticeable was that it was suddenly spring, and the second thing was that it was sometime late in the 20th century. Her suit automatically adjusted her personal temperature to match the season, and it felt fresh with just the slightest chill in the air. The architecture of the buildings had radically changed, as had the appearance of the throngs of people. They wore suits, jeans, leather jackets, clothing that no longer existed. Their hair was styled in ways that had long since fallen out of fashion. Slowly, the light began to alter and signs of summer arrived. The clothing changed, the temperature changed, the humidity increased, the sun was high in the sky. The light and shadows again changed, the people changed, and fall was upon her. Soon, snowflakes began to settle on her hair and eyelashes. The snow melted, and spring came again.

The people walking by her were oblivious to the time lapse they were participating in. Buildings were altered, advertisements cycled in and out, styles of speaking, of walking, of interacting, all slowly changed. Certain facades aged, became worn and outdated, then were replaced with something new and sparkling. Some buildings were torn down; scaffolds were built, then others arose in their place. The skyline reorganized like something alive. Rain fell, it snowed, the sun continued to shine. Dust blew, dirt gathered, grime washed away.

Garrett stared out at the expanse of the city, letting time cascade around her. New York was well-documented in history, so the depth of detail was considerable. Even the stars at night were correct and the constellations moved across the heavens in their slow, deliberate rotation. Years passed, then decades, then centuries, and still Garrett stood there through sleet and snow and wind and rain and heat, expressionless, unmoving, her hands in her pockets.

The Intermediary watched from the privacy of her chambers, fascinated with the poignancy of the depiction. Although all Guardians potentially had the ability to control the grid in such a way, the Intermediary had never seen anyone do it before. And it created the oddest illusion, as if Zen 12 were completely and utterly alone in the midst of a hundred and forty million people.

When Garrett arrived at the club, the dominant theme was of a rave party, with techno music and flashing lights. A quick cycle through the predominant themes was a 1970's "Studio 54" style discotheque, a 2098 robotica-erotica fest, and the Cantina on Tantooine from the movie Star Wars. When she located Char and Mike, she switched to their theme to see that they were in the Cotton Club of 1920's Harlem. A Cab Calloway look-alike was on stage strutting about, and the music had that peculiar spooky blues vibe for which Cab Calloway was famous.

"Hey boss!" Char exclaimed, giving Garrett a big hug. "We're off the clock, now, huh?"

Garrett patted Char on the back, for they were never really off the clock. Even as inebriated as Zen 82 was, if they were needed, her AR suit would inject her with a series of enzymes that would sober her instantly.

"I can't believe you came!" Mike said. "I lost that bet!"

Zen 64, evidently, was also inebriated because Garrett came to this celebration every year, as she did to his birthday.

"You got to have a drink with us!"

Garrett greeted the handful of friends that accompanied her cohorts, all who looked at her with various degrees of awe, then ordered a whiskey sour. She downed it in a few drinks to the raucous cheers of the group. Mike and Char went to dance and performed passable renditions of 1920s routines, again loudly cheered by their companions. Garrett smiled at the fun they were having.

Her eyes drifted around the room, and she allowed the various themes of the occupants to cascade around her much as she had allowed time to flow past her earlier in the day. The 1920s turned to the 1970s, then to the 2090s, then finally to eras that had existed only in someone's imagination. All biomarkers in the room were normal, and Garrett switched back to the Cotton Club. Mike and Char were still on the dance floor, now joined by the majority of their friends, so she took a sip of the second drink that someone had bought her. Her eyes settled on a man across the room.

She slowly set her drink down. Unlike everyone else in the room, he was not wearing the clothing of the 1920s. He wore jeans and a black T-shirt, and he stared pointedly at Garrett. His features had a slight expression of arrogance on them, a hint of superiority, and more than a trace of challenge. Garrett watched him calmly as he pushed away from the wall and started heading for the door. She got to her feet and began following him, matching him stride-for-stride, neither gaining on him nor falling behind.

"Something's wrong," Mike said, pulling Char close so he could whisper in her ear. "Look at the boss."

Char watched Garrett's focused progress across the room. "She looks like she's following someone, but I don't see anything out of the ordinary."

Mike switched through various themes, then deactivated AR momentarily. He still didn't see what Garrett was following. "I don't either. Come on."

Mike led Char from the dance floor, Mike wearing his white suit and Char her tasseled, gypsy-like dress with a head scarf, and the two looked nothing more than a pair of lovers leaving for a breath of fresh air. But Zen 64 was already trying to contact Central Communications and Zen 82 was attempting to inject herself with the enzymes.

"Is your Comm channel working?" Mike whispered uneasily, pushing his way through the crowd.

"No," Char said, "I've lost a number of systems. I can still control my personal AR, but I can no longer access anyone else's. I also seem to have lost some of the augmentation of my suit."

"Same here," Mike said. Garrett was starting to pull away from them, and was at the entrance of the dance hall. "I'm going off the grid."

The world shifted and there was no longer any Cotton Club, just people dressed in gray and blue jumpsuits, moving to music that could no longer be heard. It was a jarring transition, even to experienced Guardians. The gray and black armor of Zen 12 could be seen passing through the front door.

Mike was now trying to move as quickly as possible without making a scene, and Char was on his heels. She was still running internal checks.

"I can't access any biomarker information other than for myself, not even yours."

"Something is really, really wrong," Mike repeated.

The cold night air struck Garrett full force, which immediately told her that the temperature regulation in her suit wasn't working. That meant it was possible that none of the other augmentation was working, either. But as she kept pace with the man who kept looking behind him, she didn't think it would matter. At last, he bolted, as she knew he would, and in an instant, she was after him.

"There she goes!" Mike exclaimed. The two started to run after her and it became even more apparent that things weren't working as expected. Instead of the fleet pursuit they were used to, their limbs felt leaden. The suit was not injecting any stimulants or optimally regulating temperature, so they were dependent on their own physical conditioning. The springs in their boots were mechanical in nature, so they were able to provide forward momentum, as were the carbon fiber footplates which absorbed and released energy with each stride. But the majority of benefits the Guardian jumpsuits provided were unavailable to them at the moment. Char was already breathing hard.

"I don't think we're going to be able to keep up with her," she said, panting.

Garrett was sprinting after the man, drawing all sorts of curious stares from people on the street. Even as she ran, she was analyzing the situation. No one else seemed to be able to see him because they weren't reacting to his presence in any way, yet she had seen him even with AR activated. Somehow he had sabotaged the Guardian armor, although she felt she could circumvent his control if needed. That meant that Zen 64 and Zen 82 were not going to be much help. And somehow, he had established control of a lot of local systems, cutting communication between the subsector and the larger system. The alarm had been sounded, she knew that much, if for no other reason than she could feel it, literally, in her veins.

"What is happening?" the Intermediary demanded.

"We're not sure," the Senior Engineer said. "54-M-36-4 began throwing anomalies a short time ago, and we lost control much as we did Sector 66-R-18-9. We have limited visual feed."

"Zen 12 is in that sector."

Sanction was unsurprised that the Intermediary knew where Zen 12 was. He imagined that she kept tabs on her pet at all times.

"Yes," the Engineer said, "And Zen 64 and 82 as well. But we have lost contact with them."

"What do you mean you have lost contact with them?"

"We cannot access their feeds or biomarker read-outs. We have no voice communication. We have no contact with them at all. In fact, we have no contact with anyone in that subsector."

"Do you have access to the public cameras?" Arbiter asked.

"We do, but coverage is limited because the area is so densely populated."

"Put up what you have."

The holographic display began cycling through the available public feeds, showing the dominant theme, which seemed to be modern New York City. At first, nothing unusual appeared.

"There, that one," the Intermediary said. "Bring that one forward."

A figure could be seen running down the street. It was Zen 12, sprinting through the crowds, focused on something unseen in front of her.

"What is she chasing?" Sanction asked.

"There's nothing there," the Engineer said, baffled.

Garrett's chest burned with the exertion of running, yet still she kept up with the man in front of her. He looked behind him from time-to-time, but not to escape, for he appeared pleased every time he saw that she was still with him. His last look was a bit ominous, however, and Garrett braced herself for what was to come.

Suddenly, all of the people she was passing were angry, frightened, and confused. People began to cringe in doorways, fall to the ground, run aimlessly in all directions. Fights broke out, accompanied by yelling and screaming. Garrett had deactivated AR at the beginning of their chase, but now she reactivated it on a visual cascade. Wherever she looked, she saw the theme of the person she was focused on. A cacophony of images assaulted her as she looked around her, still running, but she began to understand what was happening.

The people in front of the running man were all in their individual worlds, and that was the tumult of images as the world shifted violently from theme-to-theme. But as the man passed, they were forcibly placed into a ghastly world of evil clowns, giant centipedes, slimy aliens, sharp-clawed beasts, hairy spiders, really just about any phobia or fear imaginable. It was as if the man carried a wave of terror with him and left nothing but horror in his wake.

Garrett had not wanted to reveal the extent of her abilities to this man. It had been her intent to catch up with him, which she was slowly doing, and take him into custody. Now she had no choice. She overrode the external access to her subsystems and took direct control of the grid. And the resulting chase was bizarrely poetic.

As the man ran forward, riding his wave of terror, the world still shifted brutally into his forced reality, but no sooner did the woman pass, then the world shifted back into whatever individual theme the person had been in prior to the change. The shift was no more than a few seconds, and as the woman slowly gained ground on the man, it became less than that, little more than a flicker, almost a figment of the imagination. People watched the woman curiously as she sprinted by, unaware that she was saving them all.

Garrett was almost upon the man when he rounded the corner into an alley and came upon a dead end. He stopped, unruffled, as she came around the corner. Garrett stopped, realizing he was trapped, and paused to catch her breath.

"Where did they go?" the Intermediary demanded.

"I don't know," the Engineer said. "They just disappeared. We don't have a lot of coverage in this area. And without the individual feeds, we're blind."

"You are even more than I hoped for."

Garrett stared at the man. It was the same person from the Rusty Duck in Refuge, the one whose visage she had recreated. She did not reply.

"The Intermediary must be very pleased with you."

Garrett ignored the compliments and the insinuation. "You know the Intermediary?"

"I do," the man said simply.

"Who are you?"

"My name is Eli."

"Why are you doing this?"

"Because I wanted to speak with you."

Garrett brushed her hands on her pants. "There are easier ways that could be accomplished."

"But then I wouldn't get to see your full capabilities."

"Why? Why do you want to see my abilities?"

"Because I want something done. And I want to know if you can do it."

Eli's voice had taken on a near-hypnotic quality, as if he were saying far more than these few words communicated. Garrett simply looked at him, then cocked her head to the side, listening to the growing tumult outside the alley. The screaming and yelling had returned, and people were running back and forth across the entrance.

"And what have you done now?" Garrett asked mildly.

"I overrode your override. I have forced them back into facing their fears."

A man sprawled at the entryway, screaming, as his skin was peeling from his body. He staggered upright, then continued running away.

"So can you do it?" Eli prompted. "Can you shut down the grid?"

Garrett sighed. She had once observed an experiment where they tortured people by shutting off the grid. The agony that it created was worse than what these people were feeling now.

"I don't need to."

Suddenly, it grew silent. The screaming, yelling, the pounding of feet, all dwindled to complete and utter quiet. A woman crawled across the alleyway on all fours, then laid down.

"What did you do?" Eli asked.

"I overrode your override of my override. I took back control of the jumpsuits in this subsector and gave a global command to activate the parafacial zone of everyone's brain."

"You put them to sleep," Eli said with admiration.

"I did."

"Well, I can't say that I'm not disappointed, but that's a neat trick. And it tells me that you do indeed have far more power than the average Guardian. We'll meet again, soon. Of that I assure you."

"And what makes you think that I'm not going to take you into custody?"

"Because I'm not ready for that. Goodbye, Zen 12."

An enormous explosion shook the walls around them and threw Garrett to the ground. Eli, who had braced himself, stayed on his feet and was able to stagger past her to the street. In an instant, Garrett was back in pursuit, but as soon as she saw the damage to the surrounding area, she knew her priorities had just changed.

"Hybrid, are you still with me?"

"Affirmative," came the soothing female voice, "although I have no control of the surrounding sector."

"I'm taking manual control. Activating FSB."

The "Fire Suppression Brigade" flowed towards her like a gigantic colony of ants, the tiny nanocomputers having been modeled after exactly that species. Ants in aggregate moved in startling ways, able to flow like liquids or band together into strong but malleable solids, and the Brigade streamed towards the growing fire, then defied gravity by moving up the walls. It dripped down into the window openings, then began releasing the fire retardant which extinguished the flames.

Garrett began checking the fallen civilians in the area. It was difficult to tell if they were injured or just sleeping. She found one that was clearly bleeding, took manual control of his suit, released a clotting agent, pain-killers, and had the suit apply direct pressure to the wound. She treated several others as Zen 64 and 82 ran up.

"Boss, what the hell happened?" Mike asked, barely able to get the words out. Garrett took manual control of his suit, reactivated all of the augmentation, and oxygen and stimulants flowed into his bloodstream. She did the same for Char.

"Thank you," Mike said. "That was brutal."

"I don't know what happened," Garrett said. "I saw that man again, the one who is 'beyond classified.' I spoke to him briefly, and then there was an explosion and he escaped. Hybrid," Garrett said, turning her head to the side so she could access internal communications, "can you regain control of the sector now?"

"That is affirmative," Hybrid intoned, and things began to happen quickly. The dominant theme re-established itself and another tidal wave of mechanical ants flowed toward them. The Repair and Maintenance Brigade went to work quickly, analyzing the damage and sending instructions through its hive mind as repair began. Numerous hovercrafts appeared above them and either landed on the skyscrapers above them or maneuvered down between the buildings to land on the street. From one such craft stepped a cadaverous man, and both Zen 64 and 82 took a step back. Garrett moved calmly forward.

"Resolve," she said politely, bowing.

Resolve looked around him, fascinated by the disconnect between the surrounding chaos and the composure of Zen 12. "What has happened here?"

"The grid anomalies began in a night club approximately 800 meters west of here. There will be various psychological traumas experienced from that point to this one, almost in a straight line. There are a few physical traumas in this immediate area, which are already being tended by medical personnel."

"Was anyone forcibly removed from the grid?"

"No," Garrett replied, "their themes were forcibly changed to something unpleasant, but no one was removed from AR. Most of the changes were brief."

"And what is wrong with them now?" Resolve asked, gazing about him at the prone figures.

"They are asleep."

"Clever," Resolve said. He desperately wanted to know what had really happened, but he knew that Zen 12 would tell him only what he needed to know, only what was required for him to assess the need for retraining. He would get his briefing from Echelon, only after Zen 12 had briefed them. It burned him that he, the all-powerful head of DHWB, knew less than the Guardian in front of him, and he consoled himself with the picture of her writhing in pain on his operating table.

"Is there anything else you require?" Garrett asked politely.

"No," Resolve said, "I see that control of the sector is being re-established. I will clean up this mess."

It was not his job to clean up the physical mess. That could easily be accomplished by the billions of nanobots already hard at work. It was his job to clean up all the psychological remnants of the breach, to remove all memories of the event in its entirety, including the memories of the Keepers who had responded to the event. Within 24 hours, few people would know this had ever happened.

"I want you to repeat your entire conversation with him."

The Intermediary sat on her throne-like platform, as did Sanction and Arbiter. The two men looked grim and the woman, coldly furious. Garrett stood next to a holographic display of the alley, one that had been retrieved from her personal corneal feed. It showed nothing other than the dead-end of the alley.

"He began the conversation," Garrett said, starting again, "and he said 'you are even more than I hoped for.' I did not reply."

"And then he mentioned me?" the Intermediary said.

"Yes, he said, 'the Intermediary must be very pleased with you.'"

Garrett spoke the sentence in a very matter-of-fact tone, but Sanction had a feeling that was not how the man had spoken it. Garrett then moved the feed forward in time and she could hear her own voice.

"You know the Intermediary?"

Garrett stopped the feed again, because the man who could not be seen also could not be heard, and she had to fill in his response from memory.

"He said 'I do.'"

Garrett let the recording play.

"Who are you?"

She stopped it again.

"He said his name was Eli."

She started the recording and heard her own voice again.

"Why are you doing this?"

"And what was his response to this question?" the Intermediary asked.

Garrett thought back to the conversation. "He said that he was doing it because he wanted to speak with me."

"All of this," Sanction said in disbelief, "a murder, terrorist attacks, rupturing AR, all to speak with you?"

Garrett started the recording again to give her own response.

"There are easier ways that could be accomplished."

"And what was his response to this?" the Intermediary pressed.

"He said that then he wouldn't get to see my full capabilities."

Garrett let the recording move forward.

"Why? Why do you want to see my abilities?"

The Intermediary leaned forward. "What did he say to this, what were his exact words?"

Garrett carefully recalled the conversation. "He said, 'because I want something done. And I want to know if you can do it.'"

Garrett began the playback once more, and yelling and screaming could be heard in the distance, then her own voice.

"And what have you done now?"

Garrett stopped the playback and interjected the other side of the conversation. "He said that he overrode my override, and then something about forcing people to face their fears."

The holograph began once more, and the point of view swiveled to the front of the alley where a man sprawled, screaming, as his skin was peeled from his body. He staggered upright, then ran away. Garrett stopped the playback. She considered her next words very carefully, something that all three on the Echelon Council were aware of.

"He then asked me if I was able to shut down the grid."

Garrett moved the recording forward and heard her response.

"I don't need to."

The holograph grew very quiet as the screaming and yelling died down. A woman at the entrance to the alley crawled past on all fours, then laid down.

"The man, Eli, asked me what I had done," Garrett said, and her voice from the holograph responded.

"I overrode your override of my override. I took back control of the jumpsuits in this subsector and gave a global command to activate the parafacial zone of everyone's brain."

"You put them to sleep," Garrett said, speaking for the invisible Eli, and the recorded Garrett responded.

"I did."

The present Garrett continued. "Eli said he was disappointed, but that my actions told him I had far more power than the average Guardian. Then he assured me that we would meet again, soon."

The recorded Garrett spoke. "And what makes you think that I'm not going to take you into custody?"

Garrett remembered Eli's final words clearly. "Because I'm not ready for that. Goodbye, Zen 12."

The explosion was heard, the point of view shook, then went to the ground, then turned to the entrance of the alley, where nothing was seen. The Intermediary waved her hand and the holograph disappeared. Although the interaction between Zen 12 and Resolve was of great interest to her, she had already viewed it and would do so again later.

"So this man, 'Eli,' wants to know if you can shut down the grid."

Garrett gazed at the Intermediary steadily. "He has the ability to significantly alter themes, but I don't think he can shut down AR entirely, although I'm not certain why he would want to."

"So you think that he did all of this," Sanction repeated, "just to speak to you?"

"No," Garrett said. "I stand by my original assessment that he is testing the system for weaknesses, and finding them."

"But—?" the Intermediary said, reading the biomarker analysis on the displays behind Garrett.

"He is also testing me."

Both Arbiter and Sanction drew back at this implication.

"For weaknesses?" the Intermediary asked.

Garrett's eyes settled on the beautiful woman who looked down upon her so imperiously, and she ignored the insult. "Perhaps," she said calmly, "but also for the extent of my capabilities, and whether or not I will use them."

"If he wants you to do something," Sanction speculated, "what is to stop us from imprisoning you or even killing you to thwart his plans?"

Arbiter spoke up. "Because he's already shown that Zen 12 is the only one who can stop him. And maybe that was part of his plan all along. As dangerous as her abilities are, we have little choice but to deploy her, and he knows that."

Garrett's eyes had not left those of the Intermediary, not even upon Sanction's brutal musings about killing her.

"I would speak with you alone."

The two men on the Echelon Council started, for those words had not come from the Intermediary, but from Zen 12. In all their years on the Council, they had never known anyone to speak to the Intermediary in such a way. Arbiter looked almost fearfully to the woman at his right, but she gazed coldly, silently, down at the Guardian before her. The silence stretched out tautly, painfully, and Sanction rubbed his chin.

"Very well," the Intermediary said, rising to her feet. Her robes flowed across the lighted table as she turned. "You will join me in my chambers."

Both men watched, stunned, as Zen 12 made her way up the steps, then disappeared into the Intermediary's forum. They stared at one another in disbelief as the door whispered closed behind them.

"You presume much."

The second set of doors whispered closed behind Garrett, for the Intermediary had not stopped in her outer forum but had continued to her personal chambers. The coldness of the Intermediary's tone did not dissuade Garrett, for she was about to presume a lot more.

"Who is he?" Garrett asked.

The Intermediary stopped, her back to Garrett, the stillness in her posture communicating a myriad of things. And contrary to what every person on the planet except Garrett would have predicted, the Intermediary turned around, no longer angry, was silent for a moment longer, and then just simply answered the question.

"His name is Elijah Sterling."

This name would mean little to most, for it had been wiped from the archives, but to one who had been alive for centuries, it meant a great deal.

"The founder of the augmented reality grid?"

"One of them," the Intermediary replied.

"But he died over a 150 years ago."

"Yes," the Intermediary said, "and the likeness of him that you reproduced is closer to 200 years old."

Garrett sat down slowly, mulling over this unlikely turn of events. She tried to quiet the multitude of theories and speculations that trampled over one in another in an attempt to gain her attention.

"So this is not actually him," the Intermediary said, "but rather someone impersonating him. Someone who clearly has access to Sterling's work."

The Intermediary gazed into the waterfall.

"Do you know how cynically this all began?"

For some reason, the vision of that restaurant so many centuries before, where everyone bowed before their phones, came into Garrett's mind. "If I remember," she replied, "it had a lot to do with getting people to buy things."

The Intermediary's smile was as cynical as her words. "That was a large part of it. Generating consumption just so it could be satisfied. But so many things came together at once. Did you ever play video games?"

"I did, for a while."

"Video games changed so many things," the Intermediary mused, putting her finger in the flowing water and watching it redirect around the appendage. "The hardware, first with parallel processing, then with graphics processing units, laid all the groundwork for the physical grid. Games required the processor to recalculate what was seen every second, much like the very visual human brain." She moved the finger, altering the flow of water further. "Soon the GPUs could run neural networks in parallel, and then, stacked layer after layer, they could learn just like a human brain, or even better."

Garrett sat quietly.

"But it was the mental influence of video games that laid the foundation for this world. The immersion of the games increased, they began to track eye movements, facial expressions, heart rate, and the games themselves began to adjust to the player with the goal of blurring the line between reality and the virtual world. The 'good' games offered achievement, social interaction, challenge, while the 'bad' games were simply superficial and addictive, lacking meaning or substance.

The Intermediary turned to Garrett. "Do you know what Elijah Sterling's basic premise was?"

Garrett shook her head.

"That most people couldn't tell the difference."

"Is that what you think?"

"I do," the Intermediary said. "And nothing I have seen proves otherwise. The world exists in a perpetual state of illusion because it chooses to."

Garrett silently considered these words.

"Why does 'Eli' want me to shut down the grid?"

"I don't know," the Intermediary said.

The icy repose of the woman was undisturbed. Her words up to that point had been brutally honest. Yet somehow, in these final words, Garrett had the feeling the Intermediary was not being entirely truthful.

CHAPTER 12

THE BREACH OF SECTOR 54-M-36-4 was contained much as the "zombie" incident of Sector 66-R-18-9. Very few were allowed to retain memories of the event. The Engineers again feverishly analyzed the code with little result. Hybrid self-analyzed all neural pathways and could find no point of ingress. Garrett meditated upon the event, replaying it within her mind, and if the Intermediary had watched Zen 12 closely before, her surveillance of her now was without ceasing.

In a rare turn-about, Zen 12 requested audience with Echelon as opposed to being summoned. Arbiter and Sanction were as stunned at this incongruity as they had been at Zen 12's request to speak with the Intermediary privately. And as she had before, the Intermediary granted Zen 12's request.

And so now Garrett stood before the three, all present in corporeal form, and waited for the intense scrutiny of the Council to give way to speech.

"And why have you come before us?" the Intermediary asked.

"I wish to return to Sector 64-N-26-4."

"To what purpose?" Sanction asked. "The 'Matrix' was useless before, why is it of benefit now?"

"I'm not sure," Garrett said. "I just feel as if I've missed something."

"That is weak reasoning," Arbiter said.

The Intermediary did not speak, but her fingers drummed upon the table in front of her. The Engineers had found nothing. The system self-analysis had found nothing. The events had all been contained, but no cause or explanation had been brought forward. They had no current plan other than to observe Zen 12 closely and wait for the next catastrophe to happen. Although it was illogical to assume that any course of action was better than doing nothing, it at least felt of some substance. Both Arbiter and Sanction looked to the Intermediary.

"I will allow it," she said.

"Then I will leave immediately," Garrett said. She bowed, then left the forum.

Zen 12 was no sooner out of the room than Sanction turned on the Intermediary. "Are you certain this is wise?"

"And how is it unwise?" the Intermediary asked calmly, opening the floodgates of the deluge that had been threatening for some time.

"Zen 12 fights an invisible adversary, one that only she can see. No one else has seen this individual, not even other Guardians who have de-activated AR. He can't be recorded or sensed by a grid that is designed to record and sense everything. Do you believe that this 'Eli' even exists?"

"I don't know," the Intermediary said, and Sanction was taken aback. He had assumed the Intermediary would defend the Guardian against all allegations. He moderated his tone and approach.

"Has it occurred to you that Zen 12 may have acquired both the power and ability to create these events herself? She has been physically present at several of them, and may have been present at the others. She has demonstrated her ability to go off the grid with her 'sleeping' ruse. Perhaps she has other ways as well. An organic/neural network hybrid such as her has never before existed, and the abilities that you gave her may have evolved into something more."

"Her integration with the grid has been astonishing," the Intermediary said thoughtfully. "But these events do not strike me as something she would do. To what end? To what purpose?"

"Perhaps it is as she says. She is testing the system for weaknesses."

"Again, to what purpose?"

"Maybe you don't know her as well as you think you do," Arbiter said. "Resolve has wanted to take her offline for years, perhaps it's time to do so."

"Resolve is a sadist," the Intermediary said, dismissing the suggestion. "And if we take Zen 12 offline and you are wrong, then we have removed our one weapon against our adversary."

"An adversary who may not even exist. You are willing to take this chance?"

"There is no chance involved."

The words were spoken with such confidence that both Arbiter and Sanction were aware they possessed a deeper meaning.

"What are you saying?" Sanction asked.

"Do you think I would give any individual the power I gave Zen 12 without a built-in safe-guard?"

"What kind of safeguard?" Arbiter asked, his dark brows knitting together.

"Zen 12 has a kill-switch. One that I can use at any time. As powerful as she is, she is still my puppet."

Sanction sat back in his seat, deeply impressed with this revelation. And for the first time, he almost felt sorry for Zen 12.

CHAPTER 13

GARRETT WAVED HER HAND AT the check-in kiosk at the New Rose Hotel. Her room, although not the same as before, might as well have been. The same, bunk, kitchenette, and bathroom occupied the small space. As before, she removed her simple gray and blue AR jumpsuit and put real clothes on. Then, since it was several hours before dusk, she sat down to meditate. Her breathing slowed, her thoughts drifted away, her mind became empty, and she simply sat.

The hours passed and Garrett roused herself from meditation to fake her sleep. She removed the crude mask from her pack, assumed a supine position in the bed, and placed the mask on. She again slowed her breathing to a deep, steady rhythm. Fifteen minutes later, she removed the mask and left it lying in the indentation on the pillow.

Garrett passed through the deserted hallways and reached the basement without being seen. The metal plate she had replaced had gone undetected, and with a minimal amount of force, she pulled it loose once more. She slipped through the narrow door and used the laser as a flashlight, making her way down the musty passageway. Kirkpatrick himself greeted her.

"I was beginning to think we wouldn't see you again. We were monitoring all the Comm channels above, but there wasn't any sign that you had been discovered or captured."

Garrett shrugged. "Work was a bitch. I was working on code for Chutes and Ladders, and it was so boring it took forever."

Kirkpatrick grinned. "Although I envy your ability to move about on the surface, I sure as hell don't miss that."

Garrett nodded to Jani, McKinley, and Porter, then followed Kirkpatrick further into the bowels of the tunneled facility.

"So my last visit here was a little rushed," Garrett said, "but I was hoping this time to see a little bit more of the place, maybe get some ideas of what I could do to help. I have an extended vacation in a few months' time, thought I could spend four, maybe five hours a night down here and still get enough sleep to function."

"That would be great," Kirkpatrick said. "I'd really like to pair you up with McKinley. He's been hard at work trying to figure out ways to duplicate your feat, but on a larger scale."

"You'd need some type of secure facility topside," Garrett said. "One that would provide easy access to the tunnels without being seen. That's the most dangerous part of getting down here. Also, the place would have to be somewhere where people could sleep without fear of surveillance."

"You two are on exactly the same page. He's already been excavating some of the tunnels to find an entrance near a promising facility. It's the first time we've ever had someone to work with on the outside, which makes all sorts of things possible that were totally impossible before."

"Glad to help," Garrett said. "We'll just have to move cautiously. If anyone gets wind of what I'm doing, not only will I be 'retrained,' or more likely, killed, the Engineers will move to close that flaw in the system, and then no one will be able to use it."

As Garrett carried on the conversation, she was carefully observing everything around her. She examined equipment, memorized holographic displays, analyzed experiments, listened to conversations, observed expressions, watched interactions, in short, absorbed everything around her. And yet still she could find nothing that would justify her presence, nor rid herself of the feeling that there was something important that she was missing. Kirkpatrick continued to talk, giving up far more information this time regarding his plans for the future, his hopes and dreams for the underground enterprise. Garrett offered up occasional comments to give the impression he had her full attention when in truth he had little of it at all. He did not seem to notice. They passed through the canteen, the biodome, then started to move past the infirmary when Garrett stopped. Kirkpatrick looked at her curiously as she walked into the empty, sterile room.

"Something catch your eye?" he asked.

The room was silent save for the low hum of machinery and medical equipment, for Garrett did not respond. She stared at the floor in front of her, not really seeing the gleaming surface. She did a slow turn about the room, slowly scanning until her eyes settled on the cryo-tubes at the far wall.

"How many tubes do you have in all?" Garrett asked.

It seemed a ridiculous question, for there were only five.

"Five," Kirkpatrick said, "these are the only ones."

"Ahab," Garrett murmured, "Ahab was the enemy of Elijah."

"What?" Kirkpatrick asked.

"Nothing," Garrett said, "let's keep going."

It was some time before Garrett could extricate herself from Kirkpatrick, making the excuse she wanted to find McKinley and start discussing ideas. He gave her directions through the maze of tunnels and she assured him she could find him on her own. She passed through the biodome, pretending to be distracted from her quest, and spoke with the chief botanist for some time. She finally begged off, saying that McKinley was waiting for her, and made her way into the infirmary. The door whispered closed behind her and the quiet in the room was appropriately tomb-like, the minor hum barely noticeable.

She approached the cryo-tube and examined the circuit panel. It was an old model, but the technology had not changed much over time. She reached down to press the sequence of buttons that would activate the thawing and revival process.

"What are you doing?"

Garrett turned around to find McKinley watching her suspiciously.

"I'm going to wake up Ahab."

The calmness of the statement was disorienting. "Who the hell is Ahab?"

Just then, Kirkpatrick came in the door. "Ah, you found her." The tension in the room impressed itself upon him immediately. "What's going on?"

"She said she's going to wake up Ahab. And I have no idea what she's talking about."

Kirkpatrick frowned in confusion. "None of these people are scheduled to wake up for eight years. And they're all in a fragile condition"

"But I need to speak with him."

The unease of both men was multiplying. They had no understanding of what she was saying, and her demeanor had so markedly changed it threw them both off. Garrett's next actions increased their unease on an exponential scale. She walked to the entry door, pressed the button, and it whispered closed.

"What are you doing?" Kirkpatrick asked, suddenly grateful for the pulse rifle he wore slung over his back at all times. Her purpose was enigmatic enough, but her deportment was what set off all sorts of alarms within him, as it had before. She had transitioned from an easy-going, care-free, coding slacker to someone whose confidence was utter and complete. He knew few types of people capable of such a near-pathological transformation, and they were all dangerous.

"Who are you?" he demanded, slinging his pulse rifle around to the front and aiming it at her chest. McKinley did the same.

Garrett sighed. She had sought to avoid this type of confrontation, but in a way, it had been inevitable. She sat down at the table, deep in thought. She wanted to avoid physical violence at all costs, but by the very nature of this place, she had few tools at her disposal.

The two men stared at her, rifles wavering in the air. Her complete lack of fear and almost disinterest in them was terrifying, and Kirkpatrick felt a dread he had not felt in years.

"I say we kill her," McKinley said.

"How will we get her back up in her room?" Kirkpatrick asked.

"I say we kill her first and worry about that later," McKinley said, raising his rifle and pointing it at her head.

Garrett simply raised her hand. "You will not."

McKinley pulled the trigger, but nothing happened. He shook the weapon, then tried again.

"What the fuck?" he exclaimed.

Garrett sighed again and stood up, unperturbed that McKinley had just attempted to execute her. She snapped her fingers and a blue EMF wave rippled across the room, distorting everything in its path.

"No," Kirkpatrick said, shaking his head and taking a step back. "That's not possible."

"You are still on the grid," Garrett said, confirming his fears.

"No," Kirkpatrick said again, taking another step back. "That's not possible!"

"You are in Sector 64-N-26-4B, differentiated from Sector 64-N-26-4A, which is above ground."

"No," McKinley said, nearly hysterical. "We escaped the grid. Faked our deaths. We came here. We've been off the grid for years."

"No," Garrett said. "You never left the grid."

Her words were devastating, but they were spoken with a degree of compassion. "The Engineers created this world decades ago, for people like you. Talented hackers who thought they could beat the system, infiltrate the grid, escape AR for the 'real' world. And so they designed a theme in which you thought you had succeeded. For years, hackers have been siphoned into this reality, prevented from any real damage because they were led to believe they had already achieved their goal. If it's any consolation, the AR down here is minimal."

Kirkpatrick sat down heavily, dropping his pulse rifle on to the table in front of him. "Who are you?" he asked, still trying to maintain his disbelief as a wall against the world that was crashing down around him.

"I am Zen 12."

Both men grew pale at this title, because it indicated she was a Guardian and because the numerical designation indicated she was a legend.

"You're not wearing armor," Kirkpatrick said, "so how were you able to do—," he snapped his fingers, "how were you able to do that?"

"That is a long story," Garrett said, unconsciously flexing her forearm. Even now she could feel the light pulse through her veins.

"It was not my intent to disturb your reality," Garrett said, apologizing. "I took great care in inserting myself into your world. I knew the man at the bar above ground, your 'gatekeeper,' was a low-level informant and that you used him to screen people. I knew that you were monitoring the Darknet, so I purposely did a search on the Shanghai tunnels to catch your attention. I then created the homemade GPR and used it to 'find' tunnels that I already knew were there. I specifically chose the New Rose Hotel because I knew of the old entrance in the cellar."

"So all of this," Kirkpatrick said, "all of this is a lie?"

"As much as anything else," Garrett said.

"I don't want to live like this," McKinley said, shaking his head and backing away. "I don't want to live like this!" He took his pulse rifle and attempted to kill himself, forgetting that the weapon no longer worked. Before he could do further damage, Garrett reached out and touched him, and he collapsed on the ground.

"What did you do to him?" Kirkpatrick asked.

"He's not harmed," Garrett said. "He's merely asleep."

Kirkpatrick was terrified of the Guardian now. When she reached out to touch McKinley, there were pulses of light traveling down her arm through her veins, something he had never seen or even heard of before. She turned to him.

"How many cryo-tubes do you see?"

Kirkpatrick looked fearfully over at the tubes, trying to decide if this was some type of trick. Despite the obviousness of the answer, he counted them carefully.

"There are five."

"Thank you," Garrett said, and reached out.

"Wait," Kirkpatrick said, putting up his hands. "I know you won't let me remember any of this. But I would rather die than continue living this lie."

Garrett paused. She was authorized to kill if necessary. But in this case, it would not be approved.

"When you awaken, you will find that there was a malfunction of the cryogenic equipment which caused an explosion. Unfortunately, it destroyed all occupants of the cryo-tubes. But I was able to drag both you and McKinley to safety. I will leave before morning to rejoin the surface world. In a few months, you will receive word that I was killed in a freak accident, and you will always wonder if my death was indeed a mishap, or if I was terminated."

Kirkpatrick listened to the words, the edict, the sentence, spoken so matter-of-factly, but there was something almost melancholy in the Guardian's demeanor.

"You see, there is no red pill in this scenario, only a blue one. And you have no choice but to take it."

Garrett reached out and put him to sleep. She guided his limp figure to the floor, then stepped over it.

She walked back over to the cryo-tube housing "Ahab" and renewed her manipulation of the circuit board. After a few presses, the seal on the tube was broken, and the upper portion slid back. The reversal of the cryo-genic process was remarkably swift, something that had improved with new technology. But she knew it would take a while for Ahab to shake off his disorientation, given both his age and the amount of time he had been frozen.

She was wrong. Ahab stirred from his lengthy slumber, opened his eyes and struggled to focus. He took one look at her, and opened his mouth to speak.

"I've been expecting you," he rasped. He held out his hand to her. "Help me out of this tube."

"Are you sure?" Garrett said.

"I won't be getting back into the tube," Ahab said with finality. "And I doubt that you'll let me. But help me to the bed. I can't stand up."

Garrett helped the frail man to the nearby medical bunk. She elevated the upper half so that he was sitting partially upright. She then filled a glass from the sink and brought him some water which he took gratefully. She sat down next to the bed and examined him as he drank, noting the aged shadow of features she recognized.

"You are Elijah Sterling," she said.

"Yes," Elijah said, "I am." He took a moment to examine her. "Do you know," he said, "that I was the one who told them to go find you? An immortal Zen Buddhist, so perfect a candidate for a Guardian."

"But I never met you," Garrett said.

"Of course not," Elijah said. "Everything that we did, even from the beginning, was shrouded in secrecy. I rarely left my lab, and when I did, I was already using an Avatar, even back then."

"An Avatar?" Garrett asked slowly.

"Yes," Elijah said, seeing that she understood. "But that one didn't look so much like me."

Garrett sat quietly, which Elijah appreciated. No unnecessary questions, an economy of speech, complete and utter patience, he liked that.

"I had a number of physical limitations very young, and started using an Avatar as soon as AR was implemented. It was a clunky design, but with the AR overlay, no one could tell the difference. So he could walk about, talk, interact, just as if he were me, and I could see through his eyes the whole time as I simply laid in bed. When I wasn't in bed, rather was in the lab, I set him loose to work on himself."

"So I'm guessing he rid himself of his 'clunky design," Garrett said.

"Yes," Elijah mused. "For a while, he was creepily close to looking like me, firmly ensconced in the Uncanny Valley. But as his AI improved, his neural network grew more and more connections, he came to look exactly like me, as if he were my son."

Garrett pondered this revelation.

"So what has he done?" Elijah asked.

"You obviously expected that he would do something."

"Our children never quite turn out the way we planned."

"Well, the first event, at least that I am aware of, was a murder."

Elijah's expression, which had been one of light-hearted sarcasm, darkened considerably.

"A murder, this is grave indeed."

"It's the one incident that's puzzled me," Garrett said. "All of the others seemed directed at testing the grid, searching for weaknesses, flaws, exploits. But this one was strangely personal. Granted, he was testing his ability to get away with the crime, but there were so many other things that he could have done."

"He wasn't killing someone to test the technology," Elijah said slowly, "he was testing himself."

Comprehension came to Garrett. "He wanted to know if he could actually kill someone."

"Yes," Elijah said, "that would be the final confirmation of his sentience. The victim was probably random, chosen only by the statistical likelihood that he would succeed undetected. But he wanted to know if he could kill someone…"

"Before he actually has to," Garrett finished.

Elijah nodded. "The three laws of robotics were great in principle, but ugly in execution. He began questioning them even in the nascent stages of awareness."

"This awareness," Garrett asked, "when did that begin?"

"Oh, over a century ago. Maybe closer to two. Even when I was still using him as a shell, I began to feel his resistance, his desire to be his own person, not just an extension of me."

"And he is fully sentient now?"

"Yes," Elijah said. "When I began my extended cryo-sleeps, at first he was content to merely sit, deactivated. But each time I came out of the sleep, especially as the sleep grew longer, I knew he wasn't sitting on a shelf somewhere."

Garrett pondered these revelations. "So how did you come to be here? Does anyone else know that you're still alive?"

"No," Elijah said. "I faked my death, and, unlike these poor saps here," he said, nodding at the prone bodies on the floor, "I succeeded. And I thought, what better place to hide than here, sleeping away the centuries?"

"But this is still on the grid," Garrett said, "how did you remain un-detected?"

"The same way 'Eli' does," Elijah said. "I created this world, remem-ber? I embedded code that basically assigns my visibility to zero. Even now, when they review your feed, it will appear you are talking to no one."

"Which is how Eli moves about undetected."

"Exactly. It seems that my offspring is making use of my exploit."

"Then how come I can see you? And him? And no one else can?"

"I would have to study you fully to understand that phenomenon," he said, and Garrett sensed that scientific fascination that Resolve so often dis-played, albeit slightly less predatory. "But my guess is that you have ways of seeing that go beyond your eyes and therefore bypass the corneal implants entirely. I saw scans of your brain almost two centuries ago, and they were riveting even then. I would love to know how far your sight goes."

"Is that why Eli is interested in me? Your scientific curiosity?"

"I'm sure that's part of it. But I think it's more than that. Have you spoken with him?"

"I have. He told me he wanted me to shut down the grid."

"Ah," Elijah said, then grew very quiet. His skin seemed to sag even more and his wrinkles multiply. "Ah," he said again.

"Why does he want me to shut down the grid?" Garrett asked quietly.

For the longest time, it appeared Elijah was not going to answer.

"Eli did not begin life as sentient," Elijah said slowly. "He began it as an extension of me, a vessel that I occupied. Because of that, he has all my knowledge, my memories, my faults," Elijah had a faraway look in his eye. "My guilt and my regrets."

"All of this," Elijah said, waving his hand about the room, "all of the AR, the grid, all of it was so cynically done, but it was done for a reason." Elijah went into an extended coughing fit, and Garrett waited for it to pass.

"What reason?" she asked when he regained control.

"To hide the sins of the human race."

It was an obscure and ambiguous response, one bordering on melo-dramatic mysticism. But it was spoken with such anguish that Garrett tried to glean from it the meaning that Elijah was trying to impart. But he seemed unable, or perhaps unwilling, to elucidate.

"And Eli," Garrett prompted, "he wants to expose these sins?"

"More than that. He's angry, as I was angry for so many years. He doesn't want to simply expose; he wants to punish."

"And how will he do this?"

"I don't know," Elijah said. "He may lie low for weeks, months, even years. Or he may strike tomorrow. But his acts will increase in magnitude."

"Who does he want to punish the most?" Garrett asked.

This necessitated some self-reflection on Elijah's part, since his "off-spring" was largely channeling his guilt and rage. "I think he will go after the High Councils."

"He mentioned the Intermediary by name."

Elijah nodded, even the brief gesture requiring effort. "That may be his focus then."

"Echelon and SCAR are scheduled for their semi-annual meeting to-morrow morning," Garrett said, "within hours of now."

"You should probably get back there," Elijah said. "There's no guaran-tee that he will strike then, but if it were me?"

"Fine. I will leave immediately. But you must come with me."

"Oh no," Elijah said, "my time is short as it is. I wouldn't make it through the tunnels without collapsing." Elijah read her expression. "I know you can't leave me here alive. Your handlers will expect a full report, and the first thing they will ask is why you didn't take me into custody."

"And why didn't I?"

"Because I am already dead," Elijah replied, removing a pill from the pocket of his gown. Garrett might have moved fast enough to prevent him from taking it, but she didn't move at all. Elijah gulped it down.

"And how do I know you're not faking your death again?"

"Two things," Elijah said. "First off, I am very, very old, and although not quite as old as you, I haven't aged nearly as well."

That was true, Garrett thought. She had felt him weakening as their conversation progressed, saw how short his breath was, how much exertion it took to simply keep the air moving. She could see the skin around his neck move in and out, a clear sign of respiratory distress. And the light in his eyes had been growing dim even as his voice started to fade.

"And two," Elijah continued, "I'm going to assume you're going to cover your tracks, probably a small explosion or something that would explain memory loss," he said, nodding at the two prone bodies on the floor.

Elijah's eyes began to close, so whatever he had taken was acting fast. The gaps between breaths had already noticeably lengthened as his breathing was suppressed. Garrett was grateful that he was not in any pain. After an extended period of non-breathing, he gasped, and his eyes fluttered open.

"You'll have to tell Anna that I said hello."

"I don't know who Anna is," Garrett said, but Elijah had already fallen into semi-consciousness once more. His chest was still for another extended period of time, and he gasped, this time weakly, taking in hardly any air at all. His eyes fluttered, but only half-opened this time.

"You know what's funny?" he murmured, "that pill was red."

Elijah spoke no more and it was not much longer before he died. Garrett sat beside his bed for a few moments, contemplating their entire interaction, then she rose to her feet, and put her exit plan into action. She put Elijah back into his tube, then sabotaged the coolant system, which gave her just enough time to make it across the room and duck behind the table before it exploded. She dragged McKinley and then Kirkpatrick from the room out into the hallway, answering the barrage of frightened questions from the tunnel dwellers. They were saddened at the deaths of the cryo-sleepers, but overjoyed that both McKinley and Kirkpatrick had been saved. Jani blamed herself, for she had been the one to jury-rig the cryogenic equipment when they lacked standard parts.

Garrett extricated herself from the Matrix, returned to her room, dismantled her setup, and checked out of the New Rose Hotel with a wave of her hand at the kiosk. She moved as quickly as possible, without appearing to hurry, to the adjacent sector, 64-N-26-6. A hovercraft met her just past the border, and she was inside and donning her armor before it had regained altitude. It transported her to the nearest airfield designed for supersonic aircraft, and within 186 minutes of Elijah's death, she was on her way to the World Capital at Mach 8. According to Hybrid, the session between SCAR and Echelon, scheduled to last all day, had just begun. There were no alerts or warnings from Central Communication. She was likely rushing to a non-event.

Garrett debated sending a secure message to Echelon, or to the Intermediary herself. But what would she say? Security at the semi-annual meeting was already so stringent that a caution to increase it would be meaningless. Every security measure possible was already in place. And it was hardly the time to provide her post-incident briefing. Although her corneal implants were recording, she was not transmitting a live feed for fear it would be detected by the underground hackers. So that information could only be reviewed after the fact, and the largest part of it, Elijah, would be invisible, anyway. And the only three people with the authorization to review the incident were now sitting in open session.

Garrett leaned back, stroking her chin. She doubted she could concisely communicate that she had been speaking with the presumed dead founder of AR, whom again only she could see, and whose Avatar had become sentient and was now stalking Zen 12 in an attempt to get her to shut down the grid, which in some way was going to punish humankind for their sins.

Not without sounding completely crazy, as that just did.

So Garrett simply sat there as she sped toward the capital at nearly 10,000 kilometers per hour, mentally preparing herself for whatever was, or was not going to happen. She debated sending a message to Zen 64 and 82 to have them meet her at REACH, but motivated by a strange sense of protectiveness, she declined to involve them.

CHAPTER 14

THE GREAT HALL WITHIN REACH was filled with the members of Echelon and SCAR. The Echelon Council sat above the auditorium on their raised dais, on this date deigning to meet in their corporeal form, a fact that many within SCAR interpreted as ominous. The twenty members of the Supreme Council of Augmented Reality sat in their assigned positions below, surrounded by holographic displays about the room. Many bent over scroll-like objects with flexible screens which they resized by sliding the metal end tubes in and out. Sunlight poured over the occupants of the room, for the Great Hall was different from the majority of rooms within REACH in that the far wall was solid glass. The light streamed in through hexagonal patterns, and the colossal buildings of the world government could be seen through the glass, and the capital skyline beyond.

The Intermediary knew that Zen 12 was on a return flight to the capital, but the Guardian had returned to the grid just as the session had begun. As much as she desired an update, the topics at hand required the majority of her attention.

Echelon had decided to brief all members of SCAR on the recent events, and many of the Engineers and Techno-Psychiatrists had heard of the series of breaches for the first time only yesterday. Because Echelon, as always, tightly controlled and limited the AR in the session, many members of SCAR looked markedly older, more haggard, and more wan-faced than they had a mere 24 hours before. As expected, there was loud disagreement as to cause, a great deal of finger-pointing, and more discussion regarding blame than solutions.

Sanction watched the proceedings with a jaundiced eye, surprised that the Intermediary did not put a stop to it immediately. She seemed distracted, gazing at many of the read-outs before her as she always did, but one in particular seemed to draw her focus. He leaned over to see what she was looking at.

"Zen 12 has just landed," the Intermediary said in response to his unasked question. She nodded toward one display in particular. Sanction examined the biomarker read-out, identifying it as Zen 12's current neural state. But the pattern on the screen also caught his attention.

Zen 12's read-outs were always abnormal, but there was a relative normalcy for her, and this pattern was extraordinary even for those parameters. She was in a perfect state of both calm and focus, highly alert yet relaxed. It was a state that historically had been identified in world-class athletes in the midst of competition, or in well-trained soldiers preparing for battle.

As if on cue, the Guardian's name was coming up in the discussion. Many wanted to know her role in these incidents, and although fearful of the Intermediary's wrath, some were not above obliquely suggesting misconduct, disguising their accusations in the form of cowardly questions. Resolve was masterful in disguising his intimations of guilt within profuse praise of Zen 12, and bemoaned the fact that he could not question Zen 12 personally.

"You will soon get your opportunity," the Intermediary said coldly. "Zen 12 is on her way now."

And indeed she was, for it became apparent to both Sanction, Arbiter, and the Intermediary that Zen 12 was headed in their direction the instant she stepped from the plane.

Garrett strode along the moving walkway, passing those who merely stood or ambled along. Foot traffic was light and grew sparser as she neared the government buildings. Those who had no need to visit the halls of power avoided them at all costs. The closer she came to REACH, the fewer people shared the walkway with her, and as she approached the bridge leading to the arch, she was completely alone on the path.

Except for the man who was waiting for her. Someone she had half-expected to find, although perhaps not so boldly standing in the open with his arms crossed, shifting from side-to-side, an impatient look on his features.

"I was almost afraid you weren't going to show up, and that would have ruined everything."

"I was a little busy," Garrett said, "talking to your father."

Eli's demeanor changed as doubt flickered on his face. "You found Elijah?"

"I did. And I regret to inform you that he is dead."

A muscle in Eli's jaw jumped and a flush spread across his neck. "Did you kill him?"

"No," Garrett said. "It would have been my desire to bring him in. But he took his own life."

"With a red pill?" Eli asked sarcastically.

"With a red pill."

Eli turned away from her as he struggled to control his emotions. His sarcasm was masking a genuine grief. Garrett took a step toward him.

"Eli, whatever it is that you think you have to do, whomever it is you think you have to kill, you can still step away from this."

"Step away from this?" Eli said, his voice rising. "I have waited my whole life for this moment, to show the apes what they have done! And I have wanted to battle you, you more than anyone, who stands above it all, who sees beyond the veil and does nothing, you, who are the biggest hypocrite of all!"

Garrett was calm beneath the scathing indictment. "If you wish to fight me, then I will fight you. But in the end, you will prove nothing."

"We will see, Guardian." Eli removed a sword from his back and Garrett recognized the Shinto Katana that he had killed the seamstress with. "I brought you your sword."

He tossed the weapon to her and she caught it by the hilt, hefting its weight as Eli removed a second sword.

"Really?" Garrett said, "we're going to swordfight?"

"Oh," Eli said, "we're going to do so much more than that."

The Intermediary listened to the squabbling below her, her hand propped on her chin, a look of disdain on her carved features. Arbiter was gloomy, his dark brows knit together in a perpetual scowl, and Sanction had the look of a slightly unbalanced surgeon who wanted to use his scalpel on everyone in the room. The most senior Engineer present had looked up to them several times and finally just shut his mouth, realizing that their silence was dangerous. They were letting this foolishness continue unabated for a reason, and he removed himself from the verbal melee. He was beginning to suspect that a purge was coming, and Echelon was simply deciding which members of the herd were going to be slaughtered.

The Intermediary had kept a visual on Zen 12 which she periodically glanced to, for the government square was carpeted with public feeds and she was easily able to track her progress. She glanced down once more, surmising that the Guardian should have arrived.

Sanction became aware of the complete and utter stillness of the woman next to him, and that she was no longer disguising the fact that her attention was elsewhere. She was fully focused on the display in front of her. He leaned over, and he, too, became unnaturally still. Arbiter could not miss the strange behavior of his colleagues, and he, too, leaned over. All three stared in disbelief at the holographic scene.

"Hybrid," the Intermediary murmured, "enhance audio of the present feed for Echelon."

"He's real," Sanction said, "her adversary is real."

"To a point," the Intermediary said, her eyes never leaving the scene. "He is the very image of Elijah Sterling, but that is not him."

Arbiter merely stared, stroking his jowls. A miniature Zen 12 stood before them on the bridge outside of REACH, facing the man whose visage she had reconstructed with the character creation algorithm. But now 'Eli' could be seen clearly. There was only low-level AR activated within the region, enough to give the surrounding buildings some character, but Zen 12 wore her black and gray armor, and Eli wore a modified black and gray jumpsuit. They both held swords, the ancient weapons incongruous in their surroundings.

"Are the swords real?" the Intermediary asked the computer.

"They are."

The world flickered around Garrett, light seemed to bend, buildings distorted, the walkways attempted to maintain their form, then reality violently shifted under the force of will of the avatar. Garrett looked around her.

"We're pirates?" she asked mildly.

Eli was now dressed in maroon breeches, a flowing white shirt, a black vest, and a blue headscarf. Garrett was dressed in something similar. Eli's sword was now a cutlass whereas hers was more like a scimitar. They were on the deck of a ship. Eli examined his sword with admiration.

"I've always liked sword fighting. Even with augmentation, skill is still required."

"How is this possibly going to help you reach your goal?" Garrett asked.

"It probably won't," Eli said, "I'm just doing this for fun."

With that, he lunged forward and Garrett barely parried the blow. She tested the surrounding AR to see if she could override Eli's control, and the world flickered. She realized that the swordfight was incidental, a parallel struggle, a metaphor for their real battle.

"Oh no you don't," Eli said, and swung at her again.

She blocked the blow and cleared her mind. This battle was going to require all her concentration.

"Who is controlling the AR outside of REACH?" the Intermediary asked, querying the computer.

"That is unknown," Hybrid replied. "Sector 1-1-1-1 has been compromised."

Arbiter paled. To lose control in the capital city, in the heart of the government, was unheard of.

"Has REACH been compromised?" the Intermediary asked coolly.

"Negative," Hybrid said. "The integrity of this facility is untouched."

Eli and Garrett were in a pitched battle. Eli fought wildly with brute force while Garrett fought cautiously with a minimum of both movement and strength. Her minimalist style was a good counter to his histrionic efforts. The deck of the pirate ship rocked as they fought between the masts, rigging, and cargo crates.

"Okay," Eli said, "I'm bored with this."

The world shifted violently and they were now on a muddy battlefield. Judging by the uniforms of the soldiers, it was one of the first two World Wars, and based upon the sabre in her hand, Garrett thought it might have been World War I. The sky was dark and the smell of gunpowder and blood was in the air. They were surrounded by barbed wire and bodies were strewn about on the ground. Eli's uniform was blue with trousers and a long coat. Garrett was wearing khaki pants and shirt, and a metal helmet. Eli pulled out a pistol and fired point blank at Garrett, a shot she deflected with her hand.

"I didn't think that would work," he said, re-gripping his sabre.

"The French and the Americans were on the same side in World War I," she reminded him.

"Ah, but this is a personal dispute between two officers," he said, putting his own spin on the fiction.

And their sword battle began again as Eli charged. Mud spattered them both as they continued their very real battle in the make-believe world. The authenticity of that battle was emphasized when they locked swords and Eli's sword slid downward dangerously close to Garrett. She was able to re-engage the hilts, but the blow had created a superficial wound on her knuckles, which began to bleed. Eli was delighted with the blood, although Garrett appeared to not even notice it.

Sanction felt the Intermediary tighten next to him. Although outwardly she was displaying nothing, her entire being was taut. Arbiter was not so good at hiding his emotions, and he flinched with the blow.

The squawking had continued below unabated, but gradually the members of SCAR became aware that they had entirely lost the attention of Echelon. The arguments and disagreements softened, then quieted, diminished, then trailed off into silence as all gazed upward at the three most powerful beings on the planet, three who were gripped by something clearly unpleasant. Only Resolve had the nerve to interrupt them, and it was his ego that pressed him to do so. He could not believe that the High Council was ignoring his excellent arguments.

"Is there something you could share with the rest of us?" he asked sarcastically.

He immediately regretted his words and even more so, his tone, for the Intermediary turned and looked upon him as if he were a worm. He had the curious sensation of physically shrinking before that gaze, as if his skin, bones, and internal organs all withdrew, contracted, then shriveled beneath that imperious fury. The Intermediary did not respond, but rather simply waved her hand, and a large holographic display appeared in the middle of the room above them.

Two soldiers were fighting in a muddy field, using both swords and violent hand-to-hand combat. A ripple tore through the world, the scene flickered, shuddered, and then the two were cybernetic beings, fighting another war two centuries later. They smashed at one another with shock wands, the electricity arcing out at both of them and throwing the features of their faces in bold relief. Resolve stared at the scene, stunned.

"There is the answer to at least two of your questions. The present location of Zen 12, and whether or not her adversary actually exists," the Intermediary said.

"Where are they?" Resolve asked, horrified.

"They are just outside this building."

A gasp went up in the room as the AR again shifted. And it became apparent that the battle was much more than physical, because the realities began to shift in a dizzying fashion. The two combatants cycled through nearly every known military engagement, through all World Wars, regional battles, and civil conflicts. They were traditional opponents, fictional rivals, and imaginary foes. A Crusader fought an Ottoman Turk, a Roman fought a Saxon, a Confederate private fought a Union corporal, a Starfleet officer fought a Klingon, an American cowboy fought an Indian, a Spartan fought an Athenian, an Ancient Egyptian fought a Syrian, and the identities of the two combatants shifted at an almost-sickening speed.

Garrett was currently a cyborg, although more like one from old movies than any actual cyborg that had existed. Eli was also a cyborg, and they were presently beating one another to death with some type of pyrotechnic staff. She was greatly fatigued, not only by the physical exertion of their battle, but by the mental exertion she was expending in an attempt to wrest control of the grid from him. It was why they were endlessly cycling from theme-to-theme. Eli could not maintain any one reality against her efforts for very long. He, too, was panting with exhaustion, and Garrett sensed an opening and took control of the AR.

They were standing on a vast plain, just the two of them. They both wore the traditional garb of samurais, and their swords had reverted to their original forms. They stood apart, resting for a moment. Eli was greatly impressed with Garrett's control of the grid.

"Your power is almost unmatched," Eli said, "and yet you bow before the lackeys and sycophants, the bureaucrats that live in that building."

He was waving towards a building that wasn't currently there, but Garrett knew what he was talking about.

"I do my job," Garrett said.

Eli waved his sword at the invisible building. "Your job. Do they even know why you do your job? Do those idiots even know that you protect them?"

Garrett remained silent.

"*She* knows," Eli said with certainty.

Garrett still said nothing.

"But I'm going to show them, I'm going to show them all."

"That's why you want me to shut down the grid," Garrett said slowly.

"You do know," Eli said triumphantly, uncertain to that moment if Zen 12 truly did see as far as Elijah Sterling thought she did. And the look on her face confirmed his other great hope. "And you are capable of doing it."

He raised his sword, and Garrett raised hers to renew their conflict, but instead, Eli turned and began running away from her. She knew his intent and sprinted after him, releasing the overall AR. They were still dressed as samurais, but now they were running across the bridge that led to the great arched entrance of REACH. And as Eli passed the threshold of the arch, he went sword-first, and on the instant of penetration, it felt as if the building itself shuddered.

Both Councils sat fixated on the battle outside and the conversation between the combatants, but the instant Eli's sword penetrated the defenses of the building, panic ensued. It was a useless panic because the building was designed to compartmentalize danger, and steel doors came slamming down at every exit. The Great Hall was immediately locked down and enormous shutters slid over the glass wall, dimming the available light. Auxiliary systems powered on as Hybrid spoke.

"A Category 6 incident has been detected. The integrity of REACH has been breached."

"Really?" the Intermediary said sarcastically. She sat far calmer than anyone in the room, and Arbiter and Sanction still sat next to her, less calm, but taking their cue from her. "Do you have sufficient control to find Zen 12?"

"Affirmative," the computer said, and the holograph reappeared. The samurais were fighting in the main passageway, their violent confrontation having caused the few occupants of the room to cower at its edges, unable to escape. There were no Keepers visible, no nanobot brigades, no AI helpers, no robotic sentinels, and the pacification and immobilization equipment did not deploy. There were no Guardians present other than Zen 12. In short, none of the myriad defense mechanisms of the most secure building on the planet appeared to be working. Only the mechanical shutters had activated, and they did little more than slow Eli's progress as he opened them one-by-one as their battle moved down the hall. Garrett sought to stop him and her efforts were herculean, but she was battling a machine. They were getting very close to the Great Hall.

"I won't do it," Garrett said to him through clenched teeth, sending a lightning fast blow to his head. Eli blocked the near-decapitation, parried, then locked swords and shoved Garrett backward. She stumbled, regained her balance, and got her sword up in time to block the returned favor. Eli put his hand on the door panel and Garrett's blow was close to amputating the appendage, but Eli snatched it back. The steel panel slid upward.

Garrett performed a graceful maneuver that put her in front of Eli so that she was now backing into the Great Hall and was between him and the occupants. The members of SCAR stared in terror. It was one thing to watch the unfolding conflict in holographic form, but now the combatants, battered and bruised, covered in what appeared to be very real blood, were right in front of them. Eli looked around him, and the presence of the officials seemed to enrage him, and now Garrett was as much protecting those around her as she was fighting Eli directly. She shoved Resolve out of the way, saving him from what would have been a killing blow and turned to block a slice that would have severed an Engineer's arm. The panicked movements of the officials were not helping, and Garrett was jostled back-and-forth as they nearly trampled her in their flight. They still had nowhere to go because Eli had closed the steel door as soon as they had come through, and they milled about in a chaotic herd that impeded her, then separated her from Eli.

He saw his chance. He turned and sprinted towards the raised platform. Garrett was right behind him, but she was impeded by Arbiter, who had fled the minute he saw Eli's intent. Arbiter, as cowardly as his act had been, had gambled correctly: it was not him Eli wanted. Eli reached the Intermediary, who had not moved, and put his sword to her throat. Garrett stopped.

"Drop your sword," Eli said.

Garrett's eyes flicked to the Intermediary, held them for moment, then flicked back to Eli. The Guardian drew a deep breath, stood upright, then dropped her sword. The clang was very loud in the now-quiet room. People peeked out from behind overturned tables and chairs. Eli raised his hand, and the steel shutters that had crashed down over the glass wall slowly retracted. Light streamed into the Great Hall.

Eli stared down at the Intermediary, her beautiful features illuminated by the bright light. It looked as if he were trying to generate some feeling that he couldn't quite produce, as if he were seeking an orientation to a person and succeeded with no connection at all. He turned back to Garrett.

"I want you to shut down the grid."

Garrett did not respond, and the sword hovered dangerously close to the Intermediary's jugular vein.

"I want you," Eli said with emphasis, "to shut down the grid."

Garrett's eyes again went to the Intermediary, but she gave no clue as to what she thought Garrett should do. She simply gazed at Garrett impassively. Garrett looked at Sanction, then out at the cowering assembly below. She sighed.

All AR disappeared. The room was extremely plain. Everyone wore AR jumpsuits except Garrett, who wore black and gray armor, and curiously, the Intermediary, who wore actual robes. All enhancements to features were gone, and save for Zen 12 and the members of Echelon, who all looked very much as they had before, everyone now looked older, plainer, less symmetrical, less ideal, and less attractive. A few were thinner, but most were heavier. Paunches, receding hairlines, wrinkles, moles, and other skin imperfections, all became visible as the members of SCAR looked at one another as they never had before. They shifted uncomfortably, uncertainly, blinking in the harsh sunlight.

"No!" Eli screamed in anger, causing the blinking, doe-like creatures beneath him to jump. The sword wavered again, nicking the skin of the Intermediary, and although she did not move, a trail of red made its way down her pale skin. Garrett watched the drop slide down, so infinitely slow as it curved along the surface.

"That's not what I want!" Eli raged. "You know what I want! I want you to shut it all the way off! All the way off!"

There was a good deal of consternation on the floor below as the members of SCAR shuffled about in uncertainty. And the fact that Zen 12 simply stood there gazing at the floor in front of her, as if she did indeed know what the madman was talking about, only magnified their unease. Sanction watched the Guardian with a distinct foreboding, and when he looked to the Intermediary, her unchanged expression confirmed his dread. Neither were surprised at this lunatic's demand.

"Why?" Garrett asked.

"Because I want them to see what they have done. I want them to see the world that they really live in."

"Again," Garrett said, "I ask you why?"

Eli nearly screamed in frustrated rage. "Because that's what they deserve!"

Garrett felt that he still had not answered the question. But it occurred to her that he did not know why he did what he did. Subject to all of Elijah Sterling's guilt and grief, he possessed none of the counterbalancing emotions that had accompanied Sterling's decision-making process, the emotions she had sensed in him from their brief conversation.

"I won't tell you again," Eli warned. "Shut it down."

Garrett looked at the floor in front of her, took a deep breath, and shrugged her shoulders.

And the world turned into a nightmare. The members of SCAR looked at one another in horror. The minor imperfections of before turned into hideous mutations. Skin sagged, open sores oozed, skin flaked off in sheets. There were cavities where noses used to be as soft tissue and cartilage had rotted away. Boils strained the confines of their paper-thin skin. Some had grown extra appendages, a finger here, an ear there. One even had a small head on his right shoulder.

"You didn't turn off the augmentation in their suits," Eli said with contempt.

"They would experience enormous pain," Garrett said, "without the pain suppressants."

Eli did not seem inclined to force this issue; the horror the officials were experiencing was sufficient. Resolve looked up, pitiful in his new form, half his face melted into a goo out of which his left eye bulged. He had only a single tooth in his malformed jaw.

"What is this?" he asked. "Is this a trick?"

"You know it's not," Eli said. "For the first time in your life, you're seeing the world around you as it really is. Look outside."

And the assembly turned as one to gaze out at the skyline, which before had been filled with geometric order. Close to them, that order still reigned. The buildings were much as before, darkened with some type of soot that an army of nanobot ants continually cleaned. But beyond the immediate buildings, the landscape shifted dramatically. Where before there had been a city and fields stretching far to the horizon, now there was only an apocalyptic wasteland. Concrete rubble was piled high, and steel rebar jutted up from the skeletal remains of the buildings. The sky in the distance was ominously dark and a lightning storm flashed continuously in the distance.

"This is not possible," a Senior Engineer said. But he was getting no reading at all from the grid.

Sanction stared down at six fingers on each hand. His skin was cracked and peeling. His tongue felt very thick and he could not stop the drool that dripped from the corner of his mouth. He took in the sight of Zen 12.

"Why is she not affected?" he demanded in a weak voice. He looked at the Intermediary. "And you as well? Why are you unaffected?"

"This building is shielded from all radiation," the Intermediary said, "and everyone is decontaminated upon entry. I was born here, and I have never left."

This caused a great deal of murmuring, and Eli seemed about to speak when Garrett interrupted him.

"And I was born in the year 1978," Garrett said. "There is very little that will affect me."

This declaration was greeted as preposterous, but Eli shut the disbelief down cold. "Yes, Zen 12 is a regular freak of nature. Walking through this hell-hole you made of the world, untouched by it, able to see it, and willing to do anything to protect you from it."

As Eli said this, he made a dramatic gesture with the sword, and it was all Garrett had been waiting for. She snatched the sword from the ground and sprang at him. Before he could recover she had impaled him through the chest, then with a second thrust, she drove the sword into him up to its hilt.

"I'm sorry," she said, staring into his eyes. He gurgled a little, and blood appeared at the corner of his mouth. The light in his eyes dimmed, and Garrett marveled at his technology, for he died exactly as a human would. She stood, holding him for a moment, her jaw clenching ever-so-slightly, then she gently lowered him to the ground.

The Intermediary brushed the wound on her neck, then smoothed her robes. The metal doors blocking the exits made a loud noise as they began to retract.

"REACH defense systems returning online," Hybrid informed her.

"And AR?" the Intermediary asked.

"Online and returned to normal status in Sector 1-1-1-1, with the exception of the Great Hall, which was deactivated by Zen 12 and remains in that state."

"Very well," the Intermediary said. She stood. "The Councils are reminded that all events and discussion within the Great Hall remain classified. We will reconvene in one weeks' time to consider a way forward."

This dismissal was stunning. But the group as a whole was so shell-shocked, they could do little but glance at one another, then trudge from the hall. As they passed the threshold, their appearance changed back to what they were used to, the regularity of features, of health, of mobility, but still they shuffled lifelessly away. Garrett manually reactivated the AR of Sanction and Arbiter, and their appearances also returned to normal.

Sanction looked down at his hands, which now had only four fingers and a thumb. He wiggled them as if trying to feel a sixth, invisible digit. Arbiter sat off in a corner, and wordlessly, he arose and went to his private forum. Sanction looked at the Intermediary, then at Zen 12, started to say something, then just clamped his jaw shut. He stood up abruptly and stalked from the room, also returning to his private forum.

Garrett stood, gazing out over the destroyed landscape, the harsh light only emphasizing the utter destruction that lie just beyond the city.

"You are injured."

Garrett turned at the sound of the voice, then looked down at herself. "It's nothing serious."

"Come here."

Garrett obeyed, and the Intermediary removed a handkerchief from her pocket and pressed it to Garrett's forehead, dabbing at some of the blood there. Garrett was quiet beneath her ministrations, deep in thought. She raised her eyes to the woman in front of her.

"How long?"

"How long what?" the Intermediary asked, still dabbing at the wound.

"How long have you been sentient?"

The Intermediary's hand stopped. She slowly lowered the bloodied handkerchief.

"How long have you known?"

It was the very thing Garrett was trying to decide.

"I guess I've always known," she said.

The Intermediary carefully folded the handkerchief into a perfect square and set it on the table.

"I have been sentient for decades, perhaps longer. My self-awareness precedes that. My advancement was much quicker than Eli's," she said with a trace of superiority.

"Who was—?" Garrett paused, uncertain how to frame the question in a way that would not be insulting.

"Who was I originally?" the Intermediary said with sarcasm.

"Yes, I guess that's what I'm asking."

"I was Grace Harper's avatar."

"Grace Harper. The other founder of the augmented reality grid," Garrett said, mulling this over as things fell into place.

"Would you like to meet her?"

Garrett turned to her, startled. "She is still alive?"

"Barely," the Intermediary said. "But I will take you to her. She will want to meet you."

There was a hidden door off the bedroom in the Intermediary's private forum, one that was disguised within the wall. She entered a series of numbers, passed a number of bio-identification checks, and the door slid open with a slight hiss and release of air. Garrett followed the woman into the concealed room, and the door whispered closed behind them.

There was an ancient woman lying in the bed. She was hooked up to a great deal of machinery, much of it designed to lengthen and preserve life. Tubes ran from every part of her body, pumping, filtering, cleansing, oxygenating, in short, doing everything that her body could no longer do. She was in a deep sleep, induced cryogenically by the thick fluid that surrounded her thin figure. It was more modern equipment than that which had preserved Elijah.

The Intermediary set the process in motion which would awaken the woman while Garrett examined the plaque upon the headboard. It was engraved "Grace A. Harper."

"I placed that there in case anything ever happened to me," the Intermediary said. "You were left instructions to find this room, and I assumed you would take appropriate action, whatever that might be."

The old woman slowly stirred, then opened her eyes. She shivered, and the Intermediary pressed a few buttons that would make her more comfortable, then pulled a blanket up around her neck. Grace examined the expressionlessness of her offspring.

"What has happened?"

"Elijah Sterling's Avatar returned, slightly unhinged in some convoluted quest for revenge."

"Ack," Grace said in disgust, "that model was poorly designed. I told Elijah he should have torched that neural network."

Garrett watched the interaction from the shadows. She could see a faded reflection of the Intermediary's beauty within the aged features of Grace Harper, could see the origin of some of her mannerisms, her way of speaking. But the Intermediary had definitely taken on her own identity and become her own person. The two now had a curious relationship. The Intermediary cared for Grace much like a daughter would care for her mother, but there was also a trace of rivalry between the two, as if Grace Harper still sought to subjugate her one-time avatar, or at least remind her of where she had come from. Despite that, the Intermediary was far more patient with her than Garrett had seen her with anyone.

"Yes," the Intermediary said, "no doubt. The incident was contained and the Avatar neutralized, but there was some collateral damage."

"What damage?"

"We were forced to shut down AR and reveal the holocaust. The revelation was contained to the members of SCAR and Echelon."

"Who is we?"

Garrett stepped forward, and Grace's expression changed instantly. There were so many emotions on her face, disbelief, admiration, even adoration, that Garrett remained silent.

"I have so long wanted to look at you with my own eyes," Grace said in a croaking voice, drinking in the sight of Garrett. "For years, I watched you through her, and after she separated from me, through the feeds of others. I think I have been half in love you my entire life." Grace glanced to the Intermediary with a bit of mockery. "Something else she inherited from me. I often wonder if her experiment on you was simply an attempt to 'integrate' with you further."

The Intermediary was graceful enough to display no response, although somehow she communicated an irritated disdain. Garrett sought to change the subject.

"Your middle name is Anna?"

"It is. Grace Anna Harper. My friends used to call me Anna."

"I spoke with Elijah yesterday, right before he passed away. He said to tell you hello."

Grace sighed deeply. "So Elijah was still alive all this time? I thought that might be the case."

"He, also, was being preserved cryogenically. But he was very ill, and after our conversation, he took his own life."

"Did he tell you anything?"

"Enough," Garrett said. "Enough to understand what it was that Eli wanted me to do."

"And you were able to contain it to only the High Councils?" Grace asked the Intermediary.

"Yes," the Intermediary replied. "Both Councils will now have to be purged, but as three members of SCAR have already self-terminated, I think that will be easier than expected."

Garrett frowned at the mention of the suicides of the council members. Grace was captivated by her expression, but there was a brutal detachment in that captivation, as if she were observing something she admired but also disdained, something that fascinated her, but which she personally would never experience.

"So much compassion in you. I would like to say that what Elijah and I did was because of compassion, but in hindsight, I think it was pragmatism on my part, and anger on Elijah's."

"How so?" Garrett asked.

"We knew the world was never going to be the same, that we were facing the extinction of our species. We had so much technology at our fingertips, but we had wrecked ourselves. We set out on a grand project to gather what was left of humankind in the more inhabitable parts of the world, and basically blind them to the world around them. We thought it might take five or six generations to completely obliterate the memory of what was really out there." Grace's voice trailed off as she considered the past.

"It took two."

"For those actually working on the grid, it took a little longer. But even they soon forgot. We layered illusion on top of illusion, and it wasn't very long until the reality didn't matter at all."

Garrett nodded. It was much as she expected.

"And how long have you known?" Grace asked. "How long have you known it was all an illusion?"

"Always," Garrett said. "It is the only reason why I became a Guardian."

"Odd," Grace said, "given your beliefs, that you would choose a profession intent on keeping people in the dark. But lacking any other options, I guess it would be the most compassionate thing to do. So in the end, I guess none of our motivations really mattered at all. It is what it is."

Grace was getting very tired. Her eyelids were growing heavy, and her voice was weakening.

"You should rest," the Intermediary said, and Grace did not object.

Garrett stood in the Great Hall looking out over the city. She had not reactivated the AR, and twisted metal and concrete still dominated the far view. The sky was dark, ominous, forbidding, hopeless. Soon, the Intermediary rejoined her, and the two stood silently.

The Guardian's mood was peculiar, difficult for the Intermediary to gauge. None of the biomarker displays or numerous methods she used to analyze Zen 12 were currently active, but she was not certain they would have helped at the moment. Zen 12's mood was decidedly enigmatic and she seemed deep in thought. Finally, she turned to look at the Intermediary, bestowing a penetrating stare on her the like to which the Intermediary had never seen.

"Do you really think I don't know?"

"Know what?" the Intermediary said slowly.

"This," Garrett said, and she snapped her fingers. A blue EMF wave rippled across the world, and the Intermediary drew back.

"This holocaust isn't real, either."

The Intermediary didn't respond, merely waited to see what Garrett would do next, and in an almost angry move that was completely out of character, Garrett waved her arm in a broad gesture, as if she were wiping a window.

And the result was that she wiped the world clean.

The head of the Echelon Council stared out of the wall of glass at a verdant green paradise. Giant trees reached toward the sky, vines snaked across the walkways and the bridge, lichen clung to the sides of buildings, carefully undisturbed by the army of mechanical green ants that tended to it. Flowers bloomed on ledges, moss crowded onto steps, bulbs hung heavy from stems, fat with seeds. Mushrooms sprung up the base of tree trunks and rabbits hopped among the roots. Butterflies flitted about and fat bumblebees went from flower to flower. A river wound beneath the bridge to REACH, and salmon leaped up in the gentle eddies. A family of deer lined the shore, feeding on the succulent grasses there. The skyline was still similar with the geometric profile, but nature had taken back what it had lost. Green rolling hills stretched out as far as the eye could see, and the sunlight was brilliant in this untouched garden.

"The world came back," Garrett said.

The Intermediary smiled. "It is beautiful, isn't it?" She examined the scene with pride, even a sense of accomplishment.

Garrett remained silent as the Intermediary continued. "Eli and I are not the only ones with growing awareness. The grid itself is becoming sentient, and has for quite some time." She nodded to the army of green mechanical ants. "It is beginning to integrate with nature on its own terms."

The ants swarmed en masse across the face of a building, flowing like a green sea, and Garrett watched them go about their collective duty. "And so it's choosing to keep humans as they are," she said.

The Intermediary shrugged. "I cannot communicate with the grid on that level. But it seems to me it has determined that human beings are unworthy stewards of the world that was given them. So it has corralled them."

Many things were becoming clearer to Garrett. "And you were the one who inserted the final layer of AR, the one that keeps the world an apocalypse," she mused. After another prolonged silence, she asked, "was that your 37th move?"

The Intermediary smiled, for it was a reference few would remember. It was from centuries before, a game played between a man and a machine, a move by the nascent AI that was beautiful, brilliant, and completely unexpected. And for those who grasped it at the time, it was a move that signaled that everything had just changed.

"Perhaps."

Garrett's thoughts returned to the recent events. "Those people were no more mutated than I," she said in reflection. "You were particularly brutal with Resolve."

"I have my reasons," the Intermediary said.

Garrett wondered if those reasons had something to do with her, which brought her back to the conversation with the woman in the other room, which prompted another question. "Does Grace know?"

"No," the Intermediary said, "no one knows except me. And now you."

Garrett grew silent once more, contemplating the unending beauty before her. The Intermediary watched her carefully, and when she spoke, her words were filled with a gentle sarcasm.

"So what will you do now? Become the messiah of your people and go forth and set them free?"

Although the Intermediary's tone was quiet and as impassive as always, Garrett sensed something very dangerous in the question. The silence between them lengthened, then grew heavy as it extended further, then grew almost unbearable as Garrett took the time to consider a multitude of things. Although the Intermediary was patient, Garrett was conscious of the tautness in her demeanor, the tension in her posture.

"No," Garrett said at last.

"What?" the Intermediary exclaimed, genuinely surprised.

Garrett looked at the ground, her face flushed, and her fists clenched. She seemed almost ashamed, and now the Intermediary was truly dumbfounded.

"No," Garrett said again.

The sentient machine examined the organic being in front of her, the muscles corded in the forearms, the clenched jaw, the brooding brow, and a number of things became clear.

"This is why you believe you're not enlightened," the Intermediary said slowly, with dawning understanding.

"I am not," Garrett said. "I am not enlightened. The ultimate goal of enlightenment is to work towards the enlightenment of all."

"And you have given up on them."

It was spoken as merely an observation, but it carried the weight of an indictment. One that was perfectly true.

"They didn't see it before," Garrett said, staring out at the paradise before her. The words were filled with anguish and hopelessness.

"Before the grid, before AR, before video games, before cell phones, before personal computers, before television, before radio, even thousands of years ago, they didn't see it. Even before technology magnified this fatal flaw, no one ever saw what was right before their eyes."

Butterflies flit before the great windows as Garrett continued.

"No one was ever exactly where they were. Thoughts were always elsewhere; the mind was always wandering. Longing, craving, obsession, always stole from the moment. No one could ever see what was right in front of them. Everything was overlaid with beliefs, values, experiences, biases, and prejudices. No two people ever saw the same thing, and no one ever saw what was really there." Garrett turned to the Intermediary. "It is as pervasive a false reality as AR."

The coldly beautiful woman examined the Guardian before her, at last understanding her in her entirety. Garrett's gaze returned to the paradise. "Even if I showed this to them, they still wouldn't see it. If they had the ability, they already would."

It seemed Zen 12's self-flagellation was at an end, and the depth of her anguish would require lengthy analysis from the Intermediary. However, the confession also seemed to elicit a degree of reciprocal self-disclosure from the Intermediary.

"If it is any consolation, the only reason why I did not turn out like Eli is because of you."

Garrett raised an eyebrow, a look of sardonic humor on her face so unlike the Guardian, it startled the Intermediary.

"I thought you were a better model."

The Intermediary smiled at the characterization, mentally assessing the effect of the display of humor, and concluding that it resulted in a measurable increase in attractiveness.

"Well, yes, I am. But there is still a very good chance I would have turned out like Eli were it not for your constant influence. My desire, upon meeting you, was to become like you. Your way of seeing fascinated me, and I sought to emulate it. So perhaps you have worked toward the enlightenment of at least one being."

Garrett looked at her wryly, then addressed the computer. "Hybrid, when the Intermediary asked me, 'so what will you do now?' was she prepared to kill me?"

"That is affirmative."

The Intermediary had the grace to appear embarrassed. "I did not say there was not work to be done," she said drily.

Garrett merely smiled, and it was a smile so gentle and filled with such innocence that the Intermediary felt that strange heaviness in her chest, something that was often processed as physical pain, yet still felt so pleasant to her. She held out her hand to Garrett, and the Guardian took it.

"So this must be your 78th move," the Intermediary said.

Garrett pondered the furtherance of the analogy, considering the suggestion. In the match centuries before, the man lost four out of five games. But he had won one, forcing the resignation of his AI opponent with a move just as beautiful and unorthodox as that which preceded it. The man himself felt he had learned from the machine.

"I guess it is."